THE LAST EMPEROR
OF GLADNESS

By: Alden Blake

TABLE OF CONTENTS

By: Alden Blake

INTRODUCTION:
THE KINGDOM OF FLEETING JOY

There exists, in every person, a fragile territory bordered not by mountains or rivers, but by the invisible lines between memory and longing. It is a realm we stumble into in childhood and rarely find our way back to—except, perhaps, through dreams, music, or the scent of something we once loved but cannot name. This collection, *The Last Emperor of Gladness*, is a cartography of that internal country—a journey through a world where joy is both monarch and mirage, ever pursued, seldom retained.

The stories you are about to enter are not bound by geography or time. They do not cling to realism, though they often wander through streets you may recognize, or emotions you may have folded and stored away in quiet drawers. Their characters are the everyday haunted—by hope, by grief, by what might

By: Alden Blake

have been—and each of them seeks, in their own quiet rebellion, to hold onto something luminous in a world steadily dimming.

Gladness, in these stories, is not mere happiness. It is not cheer or pleasure, which are easy and common. Gladness, here, is defiance. It is the stubborn flame inside the forgotten, the broken, the misremembered. It is a kind of dignity that exists without permission. The title story, *The Last Emperor of Gladness*, imagines a world in which emotion itself is a crime, where the ghost of joy lingers like contraband in the minds of the brave. But the metaphor of the Emperor appears again and again across the stories—not always as a person, sometimes as a gesture, a whisper, a childhood invention. He is a symbol of what we have lost and what we still long to crown again within ourselves.

Why stories? Because no pursuit of joy is linear. Because gladness arrives in fragments—in a laugh you thought you'd forgotten, in the shade of an old tree, in the moment someone says your name as though they truly know it. Each of these tales is a shard of a stained-glass window that might, in the right light, show you the full cathedral of feeling. Some are sad. Others absurd. A few are sharply quiet. All are in conversation with the same absence, the same ache.

You will meet a boy who builds a kingdom from newspaper and belief. A woman who waits for her son in the rustling corners of a forgotten café. A man who chases a melody no one else can hear. A painter whose portraits may or may not erase the very people he draws. A city where time is bartered and the hour of gladness is the rarest currency. In these people, you may recognize parts of yourself—or of someone you once knew and never quite understood.

The tone of these stories is not loud. They do not scream to be seen. Instead, they murmur. They wait. They ask you to pause. You will find poetry in the quiet cracks of the sentences, in the way something broken can still reflect light. This is intentional. For in an age of noise and immediacy, the act of stillness itself becomes sacred. The stories are meant to be savored slowly, perhaps read at dusk or in the blue hush of early morning, when your defenses are low and your heart is more willing to open its old doors.

The Last Emperor of Gladness is not a book that offers easy answers. Instead, it honors uncertainty, ambivalence, and longing. It trusts that the reader is a fellow traveler—someone who also remembers the feel of a summer that never came back, or a laugh that arrived too late, or the way some rooms carry echoes long after the music ends.

If there is a message, perhaps it is this: that joy is not a possession, but a practice. That even in the quietest corners of our lives, it is possible to find something noble, something small and shining. That the emperor never truly vanishes—he simply changes form, hiding in cracked teacups, streetlights at midnight, or in the curve of a familiar shoulder in a crowd.

So come with open eyes and a listening heart. These pages are not a kingdom—but they are a map. And somewhere, if you're willing, you may just find the footsteps of your own gladness, waiting patiently beneath the dust.

Welcome to the stories.
 Welcome to the empire within.

CHAPTER 1:
THE PAPER CITY

The summer that the boy began building his city, the days arrived quiet and unpromising, like blank pages waiting to be smudged. The heat came early and without warning, curling the edges of doorframes and newspaper pages alike, warping the world into a slow, wavering blur. The boy, whose name no one ever really remembered because he hardly spoke it aloud, had no plans for the months that sprawled before him like a question without an answer.

His parents, both always tired and mostly invisible, had promised something—summer camp, a week at the lake, a trip to see relatives who lived near the ocean—but nothing had materialized. They left early and returned late, and in between, the house held only silence, dust, and the distant ticking of the neighbor's wind chime.

By: Alden Blake

The boy had his own rituals. He woke with the sun, made toast he never finished, and wandered to the edge of the small backyard where grass dared not grow. There, beneath the shed's loose floorboard, he kept his treasure: a growing bundle of newspapers, tied with frayed string and smelling of ink and history. He had begun collecting them at the end of spring— quietly salvaging them from recycling bins, asking for old issues at the corner shop, lifting copies forgotten on benches. Each page was a relic, a building block, a voice from a world too loud to live in but too fascinating to ignore.

He called it The Paper City.

It began with one tower—clumsy, fragile, leaning slightly to the left—built from folded newsprint and Scotch tape, anchored by cardboard and ambition. He placed it in the middle of the garage floor, where dust motes danced in filtered light like golden secrets. From there, the city grew outward in cautious spirals. Buildings of every imagined purpose: libraries with headlines for doors, train stations woven from crossword puzzles, museums displaying snippets of war, joy, scandal, and stock market collapse. He rolled up pages into lampposts, pleated them into staircases, cut tiny windows through op-ed columns and sports pages. The comics became murals. The obituaries became monuments.

No one else knew. That was part of the magic.

At first, the paper city was a hobby—something to pass the emptiness. But quickly, it became more. It was the first thing he thought of in the morning and the last thing he saw at night, closing his eyes to imagine its skyline expanding past the borders of the garage, past the fence, the town, the earth itself.

He gave his city a name: **Gladen,** taken from the word "glad" which he'd once heard described as "happiness that tries not to be noticed." It felt right, like a secret promise whispered into an old wall.

The boy spoke to his city in whispers. Not with real words, not at first, but with breath, intention, movement. He walked the streets barefoot, careful not to collapse the corners of alleyways or towers. He made rules: No running. No loud sounds. No sharp objects. Gladen must be kept safe. For the city was delicate—both in its construction and in its meaning. It wasn't just paper. It was everything he wanted and couldn't name. Structure where there was none. Beauty pulled from discarded things. Control in a world that seemed to forget he was there.

One afternoon, as thunderclouds prowled the sky like nervous animals, the boy constructed the **Ministry of Rain**—a tall, hollow structure layered with weather reports from five different years. At the top, he glued a paper windmill that spun whenever the garage door creaked open. It became his favorite building. It reminded him that rain could be understood, even harnessed, if only one listened closely enough.

By: Alden Blake

In time, the city developed its own logic, its own seasons. Mondays were for building bridges. Tuesdays for collecting new headlines. Wednesdays for repairs. Thursdays for dreaming up new districts. Fridays for quiet patrols with a flashlight, ensuring the corners stayed clean and undisturbed. On weekends, he allowed himself to imagine what it would be like to live there, to shrink himself to the size of a thimble and wander through Gladen with no need for anything beyond what he had made.

But the world, of course, continued outside the walls of the garage.

His parents occasionally knocked on his door, distracted and over-smiling, asking vague questions like, "Doing okay in there?" or "Want to come help with the groceries?" He nodded, always, but rarely left his city long enough to notice what they'd brought home or where they were going next.

His one neighbor, Mrs. Hennelly, an old woman with a garden of fake flowers and a voice like gravel wrapped in velvet, once saw him carrying a stack of newspapers under one arm and said, "Careful, dear. Paper cuts deeper than you think." The boy blinked at her but said nothing. He liked the idea of it—paper, something so flimsy, becoming dangerous. It felt like a secret truth.

The days piled up. His hands were smudged with ink now, always. His fingers bore tiny cuts from folding and shaping. He had begun making blueprints on notebook paper, planning expansions, debating the need for a sewer system or a university or a prison. He kept a notebook filled with laws for Gladen. Rule #17: No one shall be forgotten. Rule #23: All music must be heard, even if only once. Rule #42: Sadness may visit, but must not build a house.

And somewhere along the way, he began to believe the city was watching him back.

Not in a haunted, fearful sense—but in the way a mirror watches, or a diary, or a river. Gladen became responsive. Some mornings, he swore the windmill spun without wind. He would leave one building crumpled and return to find it somehow standing again. A paper bird, cut from the business section, once reappeared days after he'd lost it, perched on the roof of the library.

Whether by magic or imagination, the city had become alive. And in its delicate sprawl, the boy found a strange kind of joy—not the loud, laughing kind that other children seemed to wear so easily, but a quiet, humming joy that lived in the space between solitude and creation.

Still, he knew something hovered at the edges of it all. A shadow that moved just outside the boundaries of the paper streets. A truth that all things, no matter how lovingly built, are vulnerable to time, to weather, to forgetting. But for now, he ignored it. He was the architect, the mayor, the keeper of gladness. The world outside could wait.

By: Alden Blake

Tomorrow, he would build a harbor.

It was a Thursday when the stranger arrived. The air was unusually still, the kind of hush that settles before a storm or a revelation. The boy had just finished constructing a paper amphitheater using concert advertisements and was standing over it proudly, imagining the ghost of music rising from its shell-like folds. He didn't hear the garage door open. He didn't hear footsteps. What he did hear—what stopped him cold—was a voice that did not belong in the world he had made.

"Very fine work. You've kept the spirit alive."

The boy froze, his fingers clutching a strip of taped headlines. He turned slowly. At the threshold of the garage stood a man—no, not a man in the ordinary sense, but something...else. He wore a coat made of what looked like interwoven parchment, stitched with golden thread that caught the dust-light like fireflies. His eyes were pale, unreadable, like pages washed too many times in the rain. His hair, silver and wild, curled around his ears as if shaped by wind.

The boy didn't speak. No one else had ever seen the city. No one was supposed to.

The man stepped forward carefully, respectfully, his boots avoiding the edges of Gladen as if he already knew where everything was. He knelt by the Ministry of Rain and smiled, not with cruelty or mockery, but with an odd sort of reverence.

"You've grown it beautifully," he said. "Most don't make it past a few towers and a broken dream. But you, young master—" here he bowed, gently— "you've honored the legacy. That is no small feat."

The boy opened his mouth, unsure whether to scream or ask for a name. What emerged was a whisper: "Who are you?"

The stranger stood, brushing imagined dust from his coat. "I am the last of the old names. The forgotten laughter. The caretaker of joy in exile. Or," he said, tilting his head, "as your city once knew me—*The Emperor of Gladness*."

The boy blinked. He didn't remember naming an emperor. Gladen had laws, customs, even holidays marked in pencil on his notebook margins. But it had never had a ruler. He had never needed one. He was the city's keeper, wasn't he?

"You're lying," the boy said, but it came out weak, a child's resistance against thunder.

The stranger chuckled softly, his coat rustling like dry leaves. "Perhaps. But if I am, then so are you. After all, Gladen exists only because you believed in it. And so do I."

He stepped further in, stooping beneath the low beam, his gaze flicking over the city's fragile sprawl. "You've built well. The sadness is hidden in the foundations, but I see it. That's good. No city is real without it. You even built a Ministry of Rain. Do you know what that means?"

The boy shook his head.

"It means you understand the cost of joy," the emperor said. "You understand it's not free. It must be shaped, guarded, mourned when it fades, and rebuilt again. You've made a real place. And now... it is time to decide whether it stays yours, or becomes something greater."

The boy frowned. "What do you mean?"

The emperor looked at him carefully, his pale eyes suddenly filled with something heavier—something ancient and cracked. "All things you love must someday face the question of permanence. Either they are remembered by others, or they are buried with you. Cities made of paper are fragile, yes. But they are also ideas. And ideas... well, they can live longer than you know."

He paced along the edge of the university district, pausing at a crumpled newspaper bench. "But for ideas to last, they must be shared. Opened. Risked." He glanced back at the boy. "You've kept this city hidden because it brings you peace. But now, I ask: will you open its gates?"

The boy's fists clenched. "You're not real. You're just in my head."

The emperor smiled. "Most emperors are."

The boy wanted to run, to slam the garage door shut and erase every footprint. But something held him still. Maybe it was the way the emperor spoke—like someone who had seen too much and still hoped anyway. Or maybe it was the terrible realization that part of him had always been waiting for someone to notice Gladen. To validate it. To walk its paper streets and whisper: *This matters*.

"But if I let others in," the boy said slowly, "they'll ruin it. They'll mock it. Or break it. Or say it's just… paper."

The emperor nodded. "Yes. They might."

Silence bloomed between them, heavy as thunder.

"But joy," the emperor continued, "cannot be kept in glass. It was never meant to be hoarded. You must decide what kind of ruler you are. The kind who builds walls around gladness—or the kind who plants seeds of it in others, even if they trample the garden now and then."

The boy looked at his city. The amphitheater. The lampposts made of rolled advertisements. The paper bird resting on the library's roof. All of it vulnerable. All of it beautiful. His hands trembled.

"What happens if I say no?"

"Then I will bow," said the emperor, "and return to exile. Gladen will remain yours alone. And you will grow older. And the city, like all quiet joys, will fade unless you keep rebuilding it—day after day, year after year—alone."

"And if I say yes?"

The emperor smiled. "Then Gladen becomes more than a summer memory. It becomes a story that walks. A joy that breathes beyond you. It may change. It may fall. But it will live."

The boy stood in the quiet garage, heart pounding like rain on a tin roof. A gust of wind stirred the open door. The paper windmill turned.

He said nothing. He only stepped aside, just enough to let someone through the imagined gates.

The emperor nodded once, a movement slow and solemn. Then he knelt, placed a fingertip on the edge of the Ministry of Rain, and whispered a word the boy could not hear but somehow understood. A soft light passed through the paper city—a shimmer, brief and impossible, like candlelight dancing across water. And when it passed, the city was the same, and not the same. Its edges seemed crisper. Its shadows deeper. Its silence full.

"I will return," said the emperor, rising. "Not as ruler. But as witness."

"Wait," the boy said suddenly. "Do others... build cities like this?"

The emperor's face lit with something that might have been sorrow or pride. "Yes. All across the world. In basements and attics, on rooftops and in notebooks. Cities of paper. Of music. Of paint. Of language. Each one born from the ache to make something joyful in a world that often forgets how."

He stepped backward, toward the door. "You are not alone. Not anymore."

And then, as quietly as he had come, he vanished. The garage was empty. But the city remained. And for the first time, the boy wondered what it would be like to invite someone in—not to visit, but to build.

He picked up the notebook of laws. He turned to a blank page. And with a pencil softened by use, he wrote a new rule:

Rule #101: The gates may open. But only for those who know how to listen.

Outside, the first drops of rain began to fall. Inside, the city of paper waited—for footsteps, for voices, for the trembling, stubborn hope of shared gladness.

The days that followed blurred like the smudged ink of a rain-soaked headline. The boy returned to the garage each morning and found Gladen unchanged— but changed nonetheless. The buildings still stood where he had left them, the Ministry of Rain still curved like a nautilus shell, the paper windmill still spun with the draft beneath the rafters. And yet,

By: Alden Blake

everything felt watchful, expectant, as if the city had
begun to breathe in his absence.

He had not seen the emperor again.

Not in the garage. Not in the corners of his dreams.
But the words he'd spoken echoed like footsteps
through the narrow alleyways of the boy's thoughts.
What kind of ruler will you be?

He tried to distract himself—built a new observatory
out of obituaries, laid sidewalks from supermarket
flyers—but each act of creation felt somehow heavy
now. The magic wasn't gone, exactly. It had simply
become aware of itself, and that awareness made
everything harder.

And school was coming.

It hung over him like a coming eclipse—the end of
summer, the return of routines, of lockers and bells
and fluorescent-lit hours. The boy imagined himself
trying to explain Gladen to someone at school. He
pictured the laughter, the eye-rolls. *You still play with
paper?*

He almost didn't return to the garage one afternoon.
He lingered at the top of the stairs, watching the dust
shift in the light, listening to the faint hum of the
outside world: traffic, lawnmowers, the distant bark of
a neighbor's dog. And in that moment, he realized that
the real world had not stopped when he'd built

Gladen. It had simply waited, patient and indifferent, just beyond the paper walls.

He went down anyway.

Gladen was dimmer than he remembered. A few towers had slumped under their own weight. The banner across the Hall of Lost Things had torn in half. Even the amphitheater, once the proud centerpiece, was beginning to curl inward at the edges like a dying leaf.

And there, at the city's heart, lay the notebook.

He hadn't touched it since the emperor left. Dust coated its spine. He opened it slowly, and the pages sighed.

There were the laws. The original ones—simple, childlike:
1. No sadness on Thursdays.
2. The river is made of music.
3. Everyone gets a second chance.

Then came the newer ones:
87. Grief may visit, but it cannot live here.
94. Paper tears, but it can be mended.
101. The gates may open. But only for those who know how to listen.

He turned to the final page. It was blank.

He stared at it for a long time, then picked up the pencil. He wrote:

102. Cities do not last. But what they teach you might.

And he sat there, surrounded by towers of headlines and folded dreams, wondering if that was enough.

That night, he had a dream.

In it, Gladen was burning—but not with fire. With light. A golden warmth poured from the windows of every building. The windmills turned faster and faster, rising like wings. And standing on the roof of the library was the emperor, coat billowing, hand raised in farewell.

The boy tried to call out, but his voice was lost in the wind.

When he woke, the garage was quiet. Gladen was still there. But it felt like the last time he would see it whole.

He spent the day dismantling the city.

Not carelessly. Not in anger. Each building was taken apart gently, folded and stacked, the way you might pack away letters from someone you once loved. He saved the best pieces—the observatory dome, the bridge of stories, the bird that had perched for weeks on the museum roof.

The rest, he put into a box.

He kept the notebook.

And then, at last, he rolled down the garage door, slowly, listening to it creak shut like the final sentence of a chapter.

Weeks passed.

School began. The boy sat at his desk and traced cities in the margins of his worksheets. He smiled less, but thought more. One rainy day, he folded a small paper boat out of his math homework and sent it floating down the gutter outside.

No one else noticed. But he did.

Sometimes he would glance at the garage door, still closed, and feel something stir inside—a flicker of what had been. The ache of possibility. He didn't open it. Not yet.

Once, he heard someone in class whisper about a "dream city" they used to imagine when they were younger, a city made of candy and laughter. The boy didn't speak. But he smiled faintly. Not at the candy, but at the *used to*.

Because he knew better.

Joy isn't always sweet. Sometimes it's fragile and sharp-edged. Sometimes it cuts you open before it lets you feel full. But it was real. Gladen had been real. And maybe that was enough.

By: Alden Blake

Years later, the boy—no longer a boy—would find the notebook again. It would be tucked inside a box of old school projects and fading Polaroids. He would sit on the floor of a too-small apartment and read the laws aloud, surprised at how much of them he still remembered.

And perhaps, if the rain fell just right that evening, he would reach for a newspaper and a roll of tape, and begin again. Not the same city. Not the same emperor. But a new echo of gladness, shaped by older hands and deeper grief.

Or perhaps not.

Perhaps he would simply close the notebook, press it to his chest for a long, silent moment, and return it to the box.

Either way, the gates of Gladen would remain—not in the garage, not on paper, but somewhere just behind his ribs, beside the memory of that summer when joy wore a stranger's face and asked to be believed.

And maybe, just maybe, that would be enough.

CHAPTER 2:
CAFÉ OF SECOND CHANCES

The Waitress and the Café

The café sat at the corner of a street that had forgotten its own name, between a shuttered tailor's shop and a florist that never opened before noon. It had no sign above the door—only a faded wooden placard etched with a steaming cup and the ghost of a name no one could quite read anymore. But the regulars called it the Café of Second Chances, and the name had stuck like the smell of roasted beans in the old wallpaper.

Inside, the café held the hush of a place that knew how to listen. It breathed in quiet sighs: the whisper of sugar being stirred, the clink of a chipped cup against a saucer, the rustle of a newspaper's page turned too gently. Dust motes drifted through sunlight that slipped between crooked blinds, painting the worn linoleum floor with gold. There was music too—barely there—faint jazz that swam beneath conversation like a memory that refused to leave.

At the center of it all was Mara.

She had worked there longer than most buildings had stayed upright in this city. Her apron had faded from olive to something between sage and resignation, and her shoes carried the soft rhythm of someone who had walked the same tile paths too many times to count. She wore her gray hair in a bun so tight it looked like a promise she refused to break.

Mara didn't just serve coffee. She studied people. She noticed the ones who stirred too long, who lingered after their cups were empty, who looked at the door each time it opened as if they were waiting for someone they hadn't yet forgiven.

She understood that kind of waiting.

Every morning, Mara opened the café at six. She unlocked the door with a small brass key, brushed the sidewalk with a stiff broom, and adjusted the chairs so that no two sat at the same angle. At six-thirty, she lit the candle on table four—the only table with a window view—and placed a white ceramic mug there, filled with nothing but hope.

That seat was for him.

He would be in his forties now, she thought. She tried not to imagine him too vividly, afraid that she might miss him if he didn't match the picture in her mind. But she remembered the way his ears stuck out just slightly, and how he never finished his toast. How he used to drum his fingers on the table in a rhythm only he understood.

He was seventeen when he left.

He had slammed the door so hard the little windchime over the entrance broke. She had found it on the floor, twisted, the blue glass butterfly snapped in two. She'd kept it anyway. It lived in her apron pocket now, a weight no one could see.

Years passed. The city changed, lost its corners, grew new ones. But the café remained, steady as breath, as grief. Some nights, Mara would stand alone in the darkened room, surrounded by empty chairs, and whisper, *I'm still here.*

Come back. Just once.

Each customer who walked through the door carried a flicker of hope with them, whether they knew it or not. Mara would glance up from behind the counter, heart hitching for a beat—*Could it be?*—only for the moment to dissolve in a familiar smile, a nod, the face of a stranger.

Still, she served them all as if they mattered. Because they did. Each of them might be someone else's lost son, or daughter, or friend. Maybe someone out there had whispered *come back* just as she had.

By: Alden Blake

She believed, foolishly and fiercely, that second chances were real. That people who left might one day return. That broken things could still be set gently back in place.

That faith had no evidence. But it had roots.

Some customers noticed the candle at table four. Some asked, and Mara would smile and say, "For someone who might come in." She never said more. Some left flowers there. Some left notes folded like secrets. Others took the seat and cried quietly into their sleeves.

The café made space for all of them.

One winter morning, a man came in who looked almost like him. Same nose, same long fingers, same faraway look. Mara nearly dropped the teacup she was carrying. Her hands trembled as she approached his table.

"Coffee?" she asked, voice softer than usual.

He nodded. "Black."

She returned with the cup and set it down without a word. Her heart was a war drum in her chest. He looked up at her then—his eyes a darker shade, his smile unfamiliar—and said, "Thanks, ma'am."

Ma'am.

Not *Mom*.

She nodded and walked away.

Still, she lit the candle the next morning.

And the one after that.

Because hope was not something you threw away when it soured. It was something you stirred back into the brew and served again, a little sweeter each time.

Some nights, when the café closed and the world exhaled into stars, Mara would sit at table four, cup cradled in her hands, and imagine him walking through the door.

She never told anyone what she'd say.

Maybe nothing at all.

Maybe just a nod. A smile. A mug of coffee placed before him, filled not with questions, but with warmth.

After all, the café didn't demand explanations. Only arrivals.

And sometimes, that was enough.

The Man Who Knew Her Name

It was just past nine when the man walked in.

By: Alden Blake

Mara had been wiping down the sugar jars—
something she did when her thoughts began to pile
too high—when she heard the chime above the door,
the new one with copper bells that never quite rang
the same way twice. She didn't look up immediately.
The morning rush had passed, and all that remained
were two elderly sisters playing cards at the back and
a teenager hunched over a sketchbook by the counter.

The man stood in the doorway for a breath too long.
She felt it before she saw it—that pause, that
hesitation, like someone testing the air for ghosts.
When she did look, her rag stilled mid-wipe.

He was tall, though his posture bent him slightly
forward, as if bracing against some invisible wind. A
dark coat clung to his shoulders, wet from the
lingering drizzle outside. He wore a gray scarf,
unevenly wrapped, and his face was framed by the
kind of beard that spoke more of forgetfulness than
fashion. His eyes were tired, but not empty. They
flicked around the café once, settling on nothing, then
everything, all at once.

And then they found her.

Mara stood still, caught between memory and
imagination.

He approached the counter slowly. There was
something in his gait—deliberate, almost reverent. As
if the tiles beneath his shoes carried weight he had no
right to walk upon. When he reached her, he spoke.

"Mara."

Not *ma'am*. Not *excuse me*. Just her name. Soft and certain.

Her hands curled tighter around the rag. "Do I... know you?"

He gave a thin smile, more apology than joy. "Not exactly."

She waited. When nothing followed, she nodded toward the menu board.

"Coffee?"

He hesitated, then shook his head. "Tea. If you have chamomile."

They did. No one ever asked for it.

She turned to make it, her hands moving on memory. The tin creaked as she opened it. The scent, dry and floral, rose like a breath from a different life. She could feel his eyes on her. Not studying—recognizing. But from where? From when?

She set the cup in front of him and watched the steam rise between them. "You said my name."

"Yes," he said quietly. "I heard it once. A long time ago."

"In this café?"

By: Alden Blake

"In a letter."

That stopped her. A stillness came over the space between them. Outside, a car hissed through puddles. Inside, time slowed.

"What letter?"

He wrapped his hands around the cup, though he didn't drink. "From someone who used to come here. A long time ago. Before he disappeared."

Mara felt something inside her rearrange, like furniture shifting in the dark. Her voice was steady, but her chest burned. "Who?"

The man looked down into the tea. His reflection wavered.

"He never signed his name. But he wrote about you. About this place. The candle. The way you always remember the sugar before the spoon."

Her hand trembled on the edge of the counter.

"I don't understand."

He looked up at her again. His eyes were not her son's. But they carried a sorrow that felt familiar.

"I found the letter in a used book," he said. "It was tucked between the pages. I was in a shop across the river, looking for poetry. The book was filled with marginalia—scratched notes in the corners, thoughts that never made it into conversation. But that letter was... different. Like a confession never meant to be read."

She didn't speak. Her throat was too tight.

"He wrote about how he couldn't come back. About how much he wanted to. But he thought it would only hurt more. He said the café was a place where time forgave him, even if no one else could."

Mara sat down on the stool behind the counter. Her legs had gone hollow.

"Do you have it? The letter?"

He reached into his coat. From an inner pocket, he drew a folded square of paper, soft with age and opened many times. He handed it to her without a word.

She unfolded it slowly.

The handwriting was his.

She knew before reading a single word. The angle of the script, the way he looped his f's, the smudge at the bottom like he had cried while writing. She scanned the first lines, her eyes blurring.

"If you're reading this, I never got brave enough. But I need you to know I remember. I remember the candle. I remember the toast. I remember you waiting."

By: Alden Blake

She pressed a hand to her mouth.

The man looked away, as if giving her privacy inside her own heartbreak.

When she finally spoke, her voice was dust.

"Why bring this to me?"

"Because it didn't feel like mine to keep," he said. "And because I hoped—maybe—it would mean something. Even if it hurt."

She nodded. A slow, aching motion.

They sat in silence for a long time, the letter between them like a bridge over a chasm too wide to cross.

Finally, he said, "I never knew him. But I think he loved you. Deeply. Fiercely. He just... didn't know how to come home."

Mara folded the letter and held it to her chest. Her eyes were closed, her breath thin.

"When did you find it?" she asked.

"Six months ago."

"And you waited this long?"

"I was afraid," he admitted. "Afraid it would break you. Or worse—mean nothing."

She opened her eyes. "It means everything."

The candle on table four flickered just then, though no draft moved. Just a quiver, like breath held too long finally exhaled.

He stood to leave.

She wanted to stop him, to ask him to stay, to tell her more. But she understood that some messengers come only once. That not all visits are meant to be prolonged.

At the door, he turned back. "He mentioned something in the letter. Said if you ever saw someone come in and order chamomile, you'd know he still remembered."

Mara's hand went to her heart again. She nodded slowly.

He left, the bells above the door ringing softly after him.

She stood in the empty café, letter in hand, the candle still lit.

And for the first time in years, Mara didn't feel alone. Not entirely.

She crossed the room and sat at table four. The morning sun spilled in, catching the tears on her cheeks.

She lit a second candle beside the first.

By: Alden Blake

Because sometimes second chances arrive not as reunions, but as reminders.
 That love doesn't vanish. It only changes rooms.

And that hope, when shared, multiplies.

The man had been gone only minutes, but the silence he left behind stretched longer than it should have. It lingered in the corners of the café, settled on the chairs, curled beneath the scent of fresh-brewed coffee and old dreams.

Mara remained at table four, the letter resting beneath her hands. She had read it again and again since he left, not to understand it better—she already did—but to feel the rhythm of her son's voice, to listen to the spaces between the words. Regret was everywhere in it, but so too was something quieter. Love, maybe. Or guilt dressed up as love.

She had no name for the man who brought it to her. No number, no story, no truth beyond what he offered. He could have been a stranger. He could have been lying. But the paper in her hands was real. That much she knew. That much she felt in the ache blooming behind her ribs.

She finally rose from the table and returned to the counter, not because there was work to do, but because that was where she always returned when life became too large. The café was her compass.

Then she noticed it.

The mug. Still full.

The chamomile tea sat untouched. The steam had vanished, the surface stilled into a golden mirror. Next to it, folded precisely in half, was the napkin. She hadn't seen him write on it, but there it was—a faint impression in blue ink.

She picked it up, heart fluttering.

It read:
"Your candle kept him alive longer than you think."

That was all.

She stared at the words, then turned the napkin over. A second line, in the corner. Slanted, rushed.

"He died two years ago."

The café spun for a moment, quietly and terribly. She sat back down.

So that was it. Her son was gone. Dead. Not simply lost. Not wandering somewhere trying to find the courage to return. Gone.

Tears came again, but they were different now—less frantic, more full. The kind that come when a curtain is finally lifted. There was pain, yes. But also something else.

Relief.

By: Alden Blake

No more imagining him suffering in some alleyway. No more wondering if he'd forgotten her name, her face, her candle.

He hadn't.

The man—the messenger—had been telling the truth, or close enough to it. But who *was* he? A friend? A stranger with a sense of mission? She would never know. Maybe he had invented parts of the story to soften the blow. Maybe the letter had found him as by accident as it had found her.

It didn't matter anymore.

What mattered was the letter had come home. That it had been delivered.

That someone had carried the weight of another man's guilt just far enough to give her peace.

That evening, Mara closed the café early.

The streets were still wet from rain, the air holding the warmth of afternoon in the crevices of stone and brick. She didn't take the bus. She walked, letting the sky darken around her. She passed the church where she once lit candles for birthdays and years of silence. She passed the bookstore her son used to visit as a boy, where he'd sit on the floor with picture books until she had to drag him out with promises of pancakes.

She walked all the way to the river, to the bench where she had once watched him skip stones. It had been their place. She sat and listened to the water murmur stories to the banks.

From her coat pocket, she unfolded the letter again. The edges were worn now, and that seemed right. Love should be carried, not kept pristine. She read the last line once more.

"If I had been braver, I would've come home. But if you ever see a man order chamomile, it means I never forgot."

Her hands tightened on the paper. "You were brave," she whispered. "Brave enough to love me from wherever you were."

The river answered with silence.

She stayed there until the sky bruised violet. Then she stood, pressed the letter to her lips, and tucked it into the hollow of a tree they had once used to hide little treasures in.

It felt like the right place.

The next morning, the café opened as it always had.

The sisters were back at their table. The teenager sketching dragons or maybe memories. The bell rang with its usual uncertainty.

By: Alden Blake

Mara served coffee with her usual grace. But something in her was lighter. A seam inside had stitched itself back together, not perfectly, but with the honesty of a scar.

At midmorning, she lit the candle on table four. Then, on impulse, she lit a second. And she kept them both burning all day.

She didn't expect the man to return. She didn't need him to. But part of her imagined him somewhere in another café, ordering chamomile, passing along stories to people who thought they had forgotten how to hope.

Perhaps he was just a man. Or perhaps he was something else—grief in borrowed clothes, mercy in disguise.

The truth didn't matter anymore.

What mattered was that second chances didn't always come dressed in reunions. Sometimes, they arrived as letters. As cups of tea left untouched. As names spoken softly across unfamiliar counters.

Mara stood by the window, watching the world pass. For the first time in years, she didn't feel like she was waiting.

She simply was.

And that, finally, was enough.

CHAPTER 3:
THE MUSIC THAT WASN'T THERE

T he first notes came to him in the depths of sleep, fragile and elusive—a melody woven from mist and memory. Julian Marlowe woke with it clinging to the edges of his mind, shimmering just beyond reach, like a song whispered through a veil of fog. He would lie still, breath shallow, desperate to capture the tune before dawn dissolved it entirely.

But every morning, the music slipped away.

He was a composer, once celebrated for his orchestral works that swept through concert halls like tides of emotion. Now, his studio felt like a mausoleum. Stacks of unfinished scores littered the floor, yellowed with age and neglect. The piano—his once-faithful

By: Alden Blake

companion—stood silent, its keys cold beneath a layer of dust.

Julian's world had shrunk to this one haunting: a melody he heard only in dreams, intangible and incomplete. It taunted him, promising beauty but eluding form. When he tried to write it down, the notes fragmented, shattered like glass under his pen.

Each attempt ended the same—empty pages, the ghost of a tune fading with the light.

His obsession grew, pulling him deeper into sleepless nights and restless days. Friends and colleagues had stopped calling, whispers of a genius lost to silence trailing behind him. He had become a ghost himself, wandering the thin line between memory and madness.

In the gray dawn of another restless morning, Julian sat by his window, gazing out over the city's restless hum. The streets below moved in currents of sound—car horns, footsteps, distant laughter—but none held the music he craved.

He closed his eyes and listened.

In the quiet between breaths, a single note hovered, pure and haunting. His fingers itched to play it on the piano, but when he touched the keys, only silence answered.

The music wasn't there.

Or was it?

That evening, Julian visited the old record shop down the block—a dusty refuge from the modern world. Vinyl and reel-to-reel tapes lined the walls, each holding echoes of forgotten melodies. The shopkeeper, an elderly man named Elias, recognized the composer's haunted gaze immediately.

"Looking for something lost?" Elias asked, his voice like gravel and honey.

Julian nodded. "Something I can't find... a melody from a dream."

Elias smiled knowingly. "Dreams are tricky things. Sometimes they're shadows of what was. Sometimes, they're whispers of what could be."

He handed Julian a thin, worn album with no label, only a hand-drawn emblem of a lone star. "Maybe this will help."

Back home, Julian placed the needle on the record. The crackle gave way to a fragile, otherworldly tune— one that stirred something deep inside him. The music was incomplete, fragmented, like his own elusive melody. But it resonated with an ache he had never been able to express.

As the last notes faded, Julian felt a spark—an ember of hope. Perhaps the music he sought wasn't lost after all. Perhaps it lived somewhere between memory and silence, waiting to be found.

Days turned into weeks. Julian immersed himself in the quest to reconstruct the dream-melody, weaving fragments of sound, memory, and imagination. He began to see the music not as something to capture, but as a presence to inhabit—a breath, a pulse, a whisper carried on the wind.

In the quiet moments between creation and despair, Julian understood that some music is meant not to be owned, but to be felt.

And in that understanding, the first real notes of the music that wasn't there began to take shape.

The melody was no longer just a haunting in Julian's mind—it was a fissure running through every corner of his life. It spilled over into his days, twisting moments with others into strange shadows of themselves. Most painfully, it reached into the delicate space he still shared with Clara.

Clara had been the center of Julian's world once. A violinist with fiery eyes and a laugh like a sudden summer storm, she had inspired some of his finest compositions. Together, their music had breathed life into concert halls and late-night jam sessions, creating a world built on shared notes and whispered dreams.

But now, that world felt distant—fractured by the silence Julian wrapped himself in. The melody that escaped him had become a wedge, pushing Clara further away with every unanswered question, every absent word.

They met one evening in a small café, the kind where soft jazz filled the air and shadows curled around old wooden tables. Clara's smile was hesitant, a fragile bridge between what was and what might have been.

"I've missed you," she said quietly.

Julian nodded, eyes tired but searching. "I'm sorry I disappeared."

She reached across the table, brushing a stray lock of hair from his forehead. "You're here now. That's what matters."

But Julian could feel the distance between them—a silence heavier than any note he'd ever composed.

"I keep hearing this melody," he confessed, voice rough. "It's like it's inside me, but I can't catch it. It's tearing me apart."

Clara's eyes softened with understanding. "Music can haunt you like that. But you don't have to face it alone."

By: Alden Blake

Over the next weeks, Clara tried to draw Julian back from his obsession. She played her violin in the quiet corners of his studio, filling the spaces with sound, hoping the music between them might heal.

Sometimes, Julian would catch glimpses of the man he used to be—the passionate composer who danced through life's chaos with a grin and a spark in his eyes. But the melody remained elusive, a ghost tethered to his soul.

Their conversations grew tangled with unfinished sentences and lingering glances. Clara wanted to help him find peace, but Julian feared that if he gave in to the melody, he might lose himself forever.

One rainy afternoon, as thunder rumbled low in the distance, Clara sat beside him at the piano.

"Let me try," she said softly.

Her fingers traced the keys, coaxing out fragments of sound—notes that didn't quite fit but shimmered with possibility. Julian closed his eyes, letting the music wash over him, feeling the fragile thread reconnect.

For a moment, the melody felt within reach.

Yet, the struggle between obsession and connection weighed heavily.

Julian's isolation deepened when Clara received an opportunity to tour with a renowned orchestra. The decision tore at both of them—a chance for her to pursue her dreams, but also a choice that might sever the fragile bond they'd rebuilt.

On the night before her departure, they stood in the studio, surrounded by silent instruments and scattered sheet music.

"Promise me you'll keep searching," Clara whispered.

Julian nodded, swallowing the lump in his throat. "I promise."

She leaned in, their foreheads touching, and in that small space, they shared a fleeting moment of hope— both knowing it might be the last.

As Clara left, Julian felt the melody grow louder, more insistent—a siren call pulling him back into solitude. But beneath the ache was a quiet gratitude.

The music that wasn't there had taught him something vital: that some melodies are not meant to be captured perfectly, but to live in the spaces between loss and love, memory and hope.

And in that truth, Julian found the strength to keep listening.

By: Alden Blake

Months slipped by in a rhythm of solitude and fragmented inspiration. Julian sat before the piano, haunted yet driven by the melody that had shadowed his waking hours and dreams alike. The music was no longer an intangible ghost—it had become a living presence, growing clearer with each hesitant note he dared to play.

He worked through countless drafts, pages filled with notes both beautiful and broken. The piece evolved slowly, a fragile tapestry of sound stitched together from fragments of memory, longing, and hope. It was no longer just a song; it was a mirror reflecting the tumult within him.

One evening, with rain pattering softly against the windowpanes, Julian played the final chord. Silence fell, thick and profound, as the last note lingered in the air before fading into nothingness.

He sat back, breath shallow, heart pounding. The piece was complete.

Tears blurred his vision as a wave of relief and sorrow washed over him. The music had been both his torment and salvation—a journey through the depths of loss and the fragile promise of renewal.

But then, something unexpected happened.

As the final chord resonated, the room seemed to shimmer and bend. The air grew thick with an almost tangible presence, as if the music itself had opened a doorway. Julian's breath caught in his throat.

From the shadows emerged a figure—ethereal, almost translucent—clad in the soft glow of twilight. It was neither friend nor foe, but something beyond description: a guardian of the music he had sought so desperately.

The figure smiled, a gesture filled with both sorrow and understanding.

"You have found it," the voice whispered, like a melody carried on the wind. "But remember—some music is meant to be lived, not possessed."

Julian reached out, trembling, but the apparition dissolved like mist before his touch.

In the days that followed, Julian felt transformed. The piece lived not only in the pages of his score but in the spaces between notes, in the silence that gave music its meaning.

He realized the melody was never truly his to hold—it belonged to the world of dreams and shadows, to the fleeting moments where joy and sorrow intertwine.

By: Alden Blake

One afternoon, Julian walked through the city's bustling streets, the finished score tucked under his arm. He passed a group of children playing, their laughter bright and untamed, and a soft smile touched his lips.

The music had taught him that the pursuit of joy is often marked by loss and longing, but it is within that tension that life finds its deepest meaning.

As the sun dipped below the horizon, casting long shadows across the pavement, Julian understood that the true melody was not a destination but a journey— a song that lives in every heart brave enough to listen.

The Music That Wasn't There ended not with a final note but with an echo—a lingering question about the nature of creation, memory, and the elusive beauty of the intangible.

Julian's story became a quiet testament to the power of hope and the courage to embrace both silence and sound, loss and love, in the endless search for meaning.

CHAPTER 4:
THE LAST LAUGH

The theater still smelled faintly of greasepaint, old velvet, and dust—the perfume of ghosts. Leo Delaney stood in the doorway, his coat clinging to his frame like a forgotten curtain on a windless stage. Outside, the demolition crew's signs fluttered against the barricades, bright yellow warnings pasted over fading posters that once bore his name in thick red letters. *Leo Delaney: The King of Late Night Laughter.*

Now, no lights buzzed above the marquee. The bulbs had been dead for years. No one cheered. No one clapped. He had returned alone, as promised.

He stepped inside.

The foyer was dim, the chandeliers coated in cobwebs, and every step echoed like a hollow joke told twice. His cane tapped the cracked tile as he moved forward, careful not to twist his knee again. They were taking it all down tomorrow, the men said. Said it wasn't safe. That the roof might give any day. But Leo had asked for this one final night. No one had argued. No one had really cared.

He passed the concession stand where he once made a teenage usher laugh so hard with a fake rubber snake that the poor boy dropped a whole tray of popcorn. He passed the heavy velvet curtains that had once parted to reveal roaring crowds, standing ovations, and nights where he felt like a god. Or at least a man worth watching.

On the stage, the dust danced under the half-light of the cracked stage bulbs he managed to switch on with trembling fingers. The spotlight—faint and flickering—still worked. Just enough. He limped to the center of the stage and stood still, letting silence wrap around him like an old tuxedo that no longer fit.

"Good evening, folks," he said to the empty seats, his voice dry but still carrying that old showman lilt. "Or should I say, goodnight?"

He let the words settle.

"No refunds tonight, I'm afraid."

The first time he told that line was in 1964, when the power cut mid-set and the crowd lit matches and lighters just so he could finish. They roared that night.

Roared. Now, the silence just watched him. He tried to smile.

Leo reached into his coat and pulled out a crumpled set of note cards. Yellowed, bent at the corners, some stained with what could've been whiskey or tears or both. He shuffled them. Cleared his throat.

"So... I told my wife she was drawing her eyebrows too high. She looked surprised."

He paused.

Nothing. No laugh. Not even the squeak of a rat in the rafters.

He tried another.

"I told my doctor I broke my arm in two places. He told me to stop going to those places."

Still nothing.

"Now that one always killed in Milwaukee," he muttered to himself. "Maybe Milwaukee just had more generous bones."

He wandered the stage, each step kicking up memory and dust. In the wings, he thought he saw the shimmer of someone watching—an usher maybe, or a fan, or some echo of the past refusing to leave. He waved at the darkness. It didn't wave back.

His voice softened. "You know, my first laugh happened right here. Not on this stage, not officially. But in the seats, fourth row center." He pointed. "I was twelve. Slipped in while the place was empty. Told jokes to the echo until an old janitor laughed and gave me a free soda. Best payment I ever got."

He sat on the edge of the stage and looked out across the faded red seats.

"They used to laugh like their lives depended on it," he said. "Like the world was ending and my dumb jokes were the only thing keeping the roof up."

He reached down, touched the floorboard where he once tripped during a skit, turned the fall into a pratfall, and made an entire room weep with laughter. It had felt like flying.

Then he heard it.

A laugh.

Just one.

Soft. Unmistakable.

It didn't come from the wings, or the balcony, or even backstage. It came from the seats. Somewhere around the third row. It wasn't a big laugh. Not one of those belly shakers he used to chase. It was more like a chuckle held back, the kind people let slip when they're surprised they've found something funny at all.

He froze.

"Alright," he said, standing slowly. "So we've got a live one tonight?"

No answer.

"Glad someone still finds me funny. Most folks these days think I've expired—like old milk with a punchline."

He laughed at himself, and maybe it was just nerves, but the air around him felt different now. Tense. Expectant. As if the theater itself had leaned forward.

He launched into an old routine—one he hadn't performed in decades. The one about the flamingo in the bar and the tax accountant. His timing was rusty, his delivery crooked like his back, but he swore he heard that laugh again. A little louder now. Closer.

It wasn't just memory. It wasn't in his head. He wasn't that far gone.

"I never figured out who you were," Leo said into the dark, wiping his brow with a trembling hand. "That laugh. I heard it once. Back in '72. Third night of my biggest tour. A sold-out show. I was on fire. Joke after joke, the room was in stitches... but then came one laugh. Just one. Didn't match the rest."

He paused.

By: Alden Blake

"It wasn't louder. Just different. Like it didn't belong. Like someone was laughing from the wrong part of the world."

He walked slowly toward the edge of the stage, peering into the gloom.

"I heard that laugh again the night I bombed in Reno. And when I buried my brother. And the night I quit the circuit. Always one step behind me. One seat away. A reminder."

He smiled bitterly. "I used to think you were death. Or madness. Or just the part of me that refused to quit. But here we are. Last curtain call."

Leo placed the cards down on the stage. Took off his hat. The lights flickered again.

He stepped forward, spread his arms wide, and bowed.

"Ladies and gentlemen, you've been a terrible audience. No clapping. No drinks thrown. Just silence. That's okay. I've had worse."

He turned.

But before he could step offstage, the laugh came again—closer, louder, full of something unnamable. It filled the theater like smoke.

Leo turned, and for a flicker of a moment, he saw a figure seated in the third row. Not quite visible, not quite there. The shape of a person. A suggestion. No face. Just a grin. Paper-thin.

The laugh echoed again, bouncing off every wall like applause from nowhere.

Leo Delaney smiled.

"There you are," he whispered. "You made it."

He stood center stage once more.

And started his final act.

The lights dimmed further, as if the building itself were trying to disappear. Still, Leo stood tall under the frail beam of the flickering spotlight. Dust swirled around him like snowflakes caught in the breath of the past. The figure in the third row remained unmoving—half-shadow, half-memory, the keeper of the laugh that had haunted him all his life.

He cleared his throat. His voice was steadier now, as if the silence were finally ready to listen.

"Tonight's set is for the forgotten," he began. "The ones who laughed and then left, the ones who stayed and forgot how. The punchlines that never landed. The ones I told just to fill the void."

He walked the stage slowly, each step a small ritual. "When you're young and funny, people think you know something they don't. That you've cracked the code of living. But all comedy is borrowed sorrow. All laughter's a secret someone wrapped in sound so it wouldn't scream."

He stopped, gazing toward the wings where the outlines of old friends seemed to shimmer in the half-dark: Benny with his big dumb grin, Josie in her sequined dress doing a sarcastic bow, and Frankie with his fake ventriloquist dummy that always made children cry.

They were all gone now. The stage held only ghosts.

"You know," he said, "we comedians—we don't chase fame. Not really. We chase that moment when someone forgets their own sadness long enough to snort out loud at something stupid. That's magic. That's alchemy. You turn grief into giggles. If you do it right, the laugh becomes a bridge between you and someone you'll never meet again."

He paused to let that thought sit, heavy and glowing.

"I remember once, early in my career, a woman came backstage after a show. She didn't say a word—just hugged me like I'd pulled her back from a cliff. I never learned her name. I just told a joke about mispronouncing 'quiche' at a fancy party. But for whatever reason, it mattered."

He turned toward the empty rows, and as he did, faint shapes began to emerge. Not real, not quite. But memories so sharp they bled. A couple holding hands, shoulders shaking with laughter. A child leaning on a father's lap, wide-eyed and giggling. An old man wiping tears from his face as he laughed too hard at a joke about dentures.

They were phantoms, yes—but phantoms of truth.

Leo raised his hand as if addressing a full house.

"Tonight's a greatest hits medley. No reviews. No hecklers. Just one old man trying to say goodbye in the only language he knows."

He launched into a routine—not his most famous, but the one that always made him feel real. It was a simple bit: a rant about trying to assemble furniture without instructions, ending with him discovering he'd accidentally built a confession booth instead of a bookshelf.

As he performed, he found himself laughing—not at the punchlines, but at the memories embedded within them. The time he slipped on a prop screw and broke his ankle mid-show. The time someone in the front row shouted, "I *am* a carpenter!" and he had to improvise a ten-minute apology in biblical verse.

He laughed until his ribs ached.

The audience of memory laughed with him. Or maybe it was just the echo. But he could almost feel the applause ripple through the room like wind through forgotten curtains.

By: Alden Blake

He took a seat on the stage floor, cross-legged like an old monk in a chapel of absurdity.

"You know what they never tell you?" he said, quieter now. "That laughter doesn't last. Not really. It's a firework—brilliant, loud, and gone before you can say you saw it."

His eyes scanned the rows again. The faces were fading now. The figures melting back into time.

"People say laughter is healing. Sure, maybe. But it's also proof. Proof that you were alive, that something touched you for a second, even if it made no sense. That's why I kept telling jokes. Because even if people forgot my name, they might remember how it felt to laugh with me."

He looked down at his own hands. The skin had thinned, veins rising like ink on parchment. Once, they had held microphones, martinis, and lovers. Now they held nothing but air.

"And sometimes," he added, "a laugh is just a scream in disguise."

The silence returned, heavier now. Like a curtain slowly falling. He felt the pressure behind his eyes, the ache in his chest—not grief, not yet. Just fullness. Like he had eaten too much of something sacred.

He stood once more, wobbled slightly, and caught himself with a smile.

"One last bit," he said, and the spotlight seemed to pulse as if in agreement.

It was a short joke. An old one. A man walks into a bar and asks for something strong. The bartender hands him a mirror. "That's the strongest thing I've got," he says.

Leo let it hang.

Then: "That one always made me feel honest."

And then he bowed—not the showman's bow with a flourish, but something simpler. Humble. A goodbye without applause.

He stood straight, exhaled slowly, and looked toward the third row again. The figure was gone. Or maybe it had never been there at all.

But just before he turned to leave, he heard the laugh one final time.

It was clear now. Crisp. And this time, he recognized it.

It wasn't death. It wasn't madness.

It was himself.

A younger Leo, bursting with hope. Laughing not because something was funny, but because it felt good to be alive.

By: Alden Blake

He nodded to the sound, then turned and walked offstage, cane tapping gently behind him.

The lights went out.

The theater held its breath.

And somewhere deep in its decaying rafters, a laugh echoed one last time—neither sad nor joyful, but true.

It was the last laugh.

And it was enough.

Outside, the wind had picked up, pushing against the theater doors with a kind of urgency, as if the night itself wanted in. Inside, the stage was empty now. The spotlight flickered twice more, then blinked out completely, leaving the auditorium in layered shadow and silence.

Leo had gone, cane in hand, steps slow but unbroken. But something had been left behind.

A breath.

A murmur.

A laugh.

It came softly at first, like the clearing of a throat. Then it unfurled—slow, deliberate, stretching across the auditorium like a thread pulled through time. It wasn't a joyful laugh. Nor was it cruel. It had no clear tone, no obvious pitch. It simply *was*, the sound of something ancient exhaling through a human mouth. The sound of something that had waited a long time to be heard.

In the third row, seat C4, where Leo had seen the figure before, there now sat a paper crown—torn at the edges, sagging slightly to one side as if tired from too many coronations. No one had placed it there. It simply appeared, and around it, the seat darkened like something had melted into it.

Then, slowly, as though time itself had grown curious, the theater began to change.

The dust reversed its fall, drifting upward toward the rafters. The decayed curtains gained a richness, a sheen, as if the years peeled backward like skin off a fruit. The chandeliers brightened with a golden glow, illuminating rows of velvet seats now suddenly upright, plush, and filled.

But the audience wasn't alive.

They sat unmoving—bodies without breath, faces without clarity. They looked sculpted from candle smoke or painted with fog. And every one of them was smiling. Wide, brittle smiles. Some twisted slightly wrong. Some impossibly serene. They didn't clap. They didn't breathe. They just *were*.

And at the center of the stage—where Leo had stood— there stood someone else now.

By: Alden Blake

Not Leo.

The figure wore the same coat, the same worn shoes, but his back was straight, impossibly tall. His face was cloaked in darkness, save for a grin that glowed faintly—wide, angular, too big for a human face, too perfect to be kind. He moved like a puppet missing its strings, head tilting in brief jerks, hands fluttering like birds at rest.

He raised one hand, and the theater responded with a creak of anticipation. In his other hand, a microphone appeared—old-fashioned, silver, the kind with slats and a coiled cord that vanished into nothing.

Then he spoke.

But not in words.

Instead, from his mouth came every laugh Leo had ever heard. A child's delighted shriek. A cruel cackle from the back of a smoky bar. The rich, rolling laugh of a man trying to hide his pain. The polite chuckle of someone who doesn't get the joke but doesn't want to seem rude. The giggle before heartbreak. The howl after fear.

The voice was layered, an orchestra of emotion. And beneath it all, threaded through every sound, was *that one laugh*—the one Leo never understood. That strange, untethered laugh that didn't belong to any moment. The laugh that echoed in the margins of his career, in the pauses between acts, in the silence after the final punchline. The one that had followed him like a second shadow.

And now, it laughed alone.

Longer. Louder. Closer.

The audience of ghosts leaned forward—not with hunger or anticipation, but as if finally hearing a long-lost friend speak.

The figure bowed.

And then the scene fractured.

The walls of the theater buckled outward, not breaking but bending into a warped dreamscape. The ceiling turned black and starless, like the inside of a sealed mind. The floor began to ripple like the surface of a lake remembering its depth.

The stage morphed beneath the figure's feet. It became a ring of mirrors, each one reflecting not what was onstage, but Leo's life—scrambled, surreal versions of it. In one, he was still a boy, chasing laughter down empty alleys. In another, he was performing to rows of open graves, each corpse clapping politely. In yet another, he sat in a silent club, telling jokes to mannequins who wept wax tears.

And always—always—after every punchline came *the laugh*.

Not as punctuation.

By: Alden Blake

But as presence.

It was no longer a sound. It had shape now. Form. It seeped through the cracks of the mirrors and curled around the figure onstage. It coalesced into something barely visible—long fingers, stitched lips, a crown made of broken cassette tape and ribbons of sound.

It leaned in, whispered into the figure's ear, and suddenly the microphone vanished.

In its place: a jester's mask.

The figure lifted it slowly and placed it over his face.

The audience of ghosts began to applaud. Slowly. Softly. Rhythmic like a ritual. The sound was not clapping. It was the soft beat of something buried waking up.

And then—

Leo Delaney stood in the alley behind the theater.

He blinked.

It was morning.

The sun had not risen, but the sky had lightened to the shade of bruised paper. The building behind him was no longer standing. It was rubble—twisted rebar and stone, scorched wood, a rusting marquee with letters half-melted and crumbling: *DELANEY RETURNS ONE NIGHT ONLY.*

Leo turned and saw his own cane in his hand. His coat smelled of dust and old velvet. He could still hear the echo of footsteps, of laughter—but distant now, like remembering the punchline of a joke from childhood.

He didn't know how he got here.

He didn't remember leaving.

He didn't know if he'd ever entered at all.

But in his pocket, he found something: a crumpled paper crown, wet with morning dew.

He held it up to the pale light.

And from the ruins behind him, just once, impossibly soft—he heard it again.

That laugh.

Not cruel. Not kind. Not familiar. Not foreign.

Just *there*.

As though it had always been.

And always would be.

Leo did not smile.

He simply bowed, very slightly, to nothing at all.

And then he walked away, leaving the crown behind in the dirt, where it dissolved like sugar into the earth.

By: Alden Blake

Back in the ruins, nothing moved.

But in the wind that passed through the broken bricks and tangled wires, the laugh lingered.

Lighter now.

Almost playful.

A breath caught between endings.

And echoes.

CHAPTER 5:
SKETCHES OF LIGHT

He only painted in chalk.

Not because it was cheaper—though it was—or because it was temporary—though that, too, had its appeal. No, Elias used chalk because it felt honest. Honest in the way a sigh is honest, or an autumn leaf: it came with the knowledge that it would not last. The rain would come, or someone's shoe, or the wind, and the colors would vanish, scrubbed clean by the careless rhythm of the city.

That was the point.

He worked mostly in alleys, quiet plazas, or on the overlooked stretches of sidewalk where no one expected beauty. Each morning he arrived at a different place, pulled the rolled-up mat from his backpack, and arranged his colors—sun-worn sticks of orange, cobalt, lilac, bone-white. He knelt, found a flat patch of cement, and began to draw.

People didn't usually notice at first. He preferred it that way.

But they always noticed when the faces started to look back.

He didn't ask them to sit for portraits. He never even spoke to them. He only watched—moments stolen from life's shuffle—and when a face held something that caught him, some slant of sorrow or stifled joy or private ache, he let it travel through his fingers.

He could draw fast, with almost frightening accuracy. Lines that looked like photographs. Eyes that seemed to search the viewer for secrets. Chalk dust beneath his nails like proof of some gentle sin.

People started coming back, searching for themselves. "That's me, right?" they'd say, half-laughing, crouching beside the sketch with something strange behind their voices. Wonder. Worry. Recognition.

And then, slowly, the disappearances began.

The first was a woman with a paper bag of oranges, caught mid-step in one of Elias's more vibrant works. Her face had been done in coral and sienna, her expression soft and haunted. He remembered her well—she had paused to adjust her scarf, and something in her eyes had gripped him like a forgotten dream.

The next morning, the oranges were still there, spilled and soft on the pavement. But the woman was gone.

Then came the man with the green umbrella. Then the child with the missing front teeth.

Elias didn't know their names. But he knew their faces. He saw them every night in his dreams, walking into silence, their chalk likenesses smeared by invisible hands.

He tried not to think about it.

People vanished in cities all the time.

Still, he started watching more carefully.

One day, after a long stretch without painting, he sat in a narrow street near a used bookstore. He had chosen it because of the light—soft, gold-filtered through scaffolding, the way it made shadows stretch like watercolor.

He began sketching a man leaning against the far wall, smoking. The man had a tired mouth and a strong brow, and Elias, working quickly, rendered him in slate gray and pale turquoise. He finished the sketch just as the man crushed his cigarette and walked away.

"Nice work," someone muttered behind him.

By: Alden Blake

Elias turned.

A girl—no older than twelve—stood watching him. Her hair was a knotted mess of curls. She wore a patched coat too large for her. Her eyes were alert in that way children's eyes sometimes are when they've had to learn more than they should.

"Thanks," he said.

She knelt beside the drawing. "That guy's not coming back, you know."

He blinked. "What do you mean?"

She glanced at him. "I've seen your pictures. You draw them, and then *poof.* They're gone."

Elias swallowed. "That's just coincidence."

She stood. "There's no such thing."

And then she was gone too, ducking around the corner like smoke.

Elias stared at the sketch, now dry and vivid in the fading light. The eyes seemed darker now. Not just shaded—but deep. Deep enough to fall into.

He didn't sleep well that night.

Dreams came thick and vivid. In one, he stood in the middle of a blank page, and the wind drew faces around him with invisible chalk. They turned to him slowly—smiling, frowning, weeping—and asked, *Why did you remember us this way?*

In the morning, he found himself at his usual corner near the fountain on Maple and 6th, where the pigeons walked like they knew every story the city had to tell. He sat. Unrolled his mat. Chose a shade of blue.

He wasn't going to draw.

He told himself this was just a ritual now. A habit.

But when the old man with the cello passed by, pausing to adjust the scarf at his neck—Elias's hand moved on its own.

The portrait emerged quickly. Hands first—gnarled and careful. Then the lines of the face, lined with time and a little music. The cello wasn't drawn at all. But it wasn't needed. The music was in the expression.

As he stepped back to look, Elias felt a shiver climb his spine.

The man turned the corner and vanished from view.

Hours passed. The sun moved on. And then came the scream.

Someone near the corner. A pedestrian shouting. A small group gathered, murmuring. Elias stood slowly, knees sore, and walked toward the commotion.

By: Alden Blake

On the ground lay the cello—its strings slack, one snapped entirely.

But no sign of the man.

No blood. No footprints. Just the instrument.

Elias didn't ask questions. He just walked away.

That night, he dug through his old sketchbooks. Years of faces stared back at him. Some he remembered. Others felt alien. But they all had one thing in common: they were drawn as if from a memory he didn't know he had.

He flipped page after page. The little girl in the red coat. The cyclist with the crooked grin. The laughing couple on the bench.

He thought of what the girl had said. *They're not coming back.*

He flipped to the final page.

Blank.

Then—slowly—he picked up his chalk.

And he began to sketch her.

The girl with the wild curls. The eyes like sharpened glass.

As the lines took shape, something strange happened.

He felt resistance. Not in his hand, but in the chalk. It cracked. Then again. And finally snapped.

He looked down.

The sketch had stopped. Half-finished. The eyes only half-formed. The hair incomplete.

But even in this state, the drawing was staring back at him.

Not passively. Not with longing.

With warning.

And just beneath the edges of the page, faint as dust, another face began to bleed through—
 not drawn, not chosen—

His own.

Smiling.

But the smile wasn't his.

It was a Tuesday—one of those featureless, gray ones where the city felt like it was holding its breath. Elias had set up shop just off Welden Street, a corner near the courthouse where foot traffic was predictable and indifferent. A busker was playing an off-key accordion nearby, and pigeons wandered in figure eights around breadcrumbs and dropped receipts.

By: Alden Blake

Elias didn't feel like drawing that day. Not really. The chalk in his pocket felt heavier, like it knew something he didn't.

Still, routine had become its own inertia. He sat, unfurled his mat, and took out a stick of ochre. He told himself he'd only draw shapes. Maybe hands. Maybe an abstract cityscape. Nothing alive.

But as he glanced up, his eyes caught on someone.

She wasn't remarkable at first glance. Maybe thirty. Tall, slight build, angular face beneath short dark hair. She was seated on the edge of a planter, staring at nothing in particular. Her expression was unreadable—calm, but not serene. As if she were listening to something far away.

He told himself not to do it. He even moved to reach for a colorless white, something neutral.

But then the wind shifted, and her coat fluttered just so, and that invisible pull—the same one that always chose for him—grabbed his hand.

And just like that, he was sketching her.

Lines first: clean, minimal. Then color: muted greens and burnt umber. Her jaw, her closed mouth, the hint of tension in her neck. He got her almost perfectly. He always did.

When he looked up again, she was still there.

But she was watching him now.

Her head had tilted. Her brows pulled in just slightly. Her eyes found the chalk, the drawing, and then his face.

She stood.

Elias froze.

She walked over. Stepped past the chalk outline. Looked down at it. And then, without blinking, said: "That's me."

He nodded, slowly.

She didn't smile. "Did you ask?"

He swallowed. "No. I never do."

"Why?"

"I don't need to."

"But you drew me. Without permission."

There was something in her tone—not quite anger. Something quieter. As if she was accusing him of something worse than disrespect.

Elias set the chalk down. "You just had... a look. I can't explain it. I only draw the ones who feel like they're already slipping away."

By: Alden Blake

The woman crouched beside the drawing. She touched the edge of it gently, as if testing whether it was warm. "That's beautiful," she murmured. "And terrifying."

She looked up at him again. "Do you know what's been happening?"

Elias went very still. "I don't know what you mean."

"Yes, you do," she said. "People disappear. After you draw them."

He didn't answer.

"I know because I've been watching you," she added. "You come to a different place each day. You always pick someone with sad eyes. And then they vanish."

She stood, brushing her coat. "Are you making them disappear? Is it you?"

"No," Elias said quickly. "I just... capture them. I don't make anything happen."

"Don't you?" she asked. "You catch something. A moment that maybe shouldn't be kept. And then it's like they've been—released."

Elias looked down at the chalk. His hands were covered in dust.

"I saw a man vanish last week," she said. "The one with the cello. I watched you finish the sketch, and then I saw him walk into the alley behind the flower shop. And that was it. He never came out."

"What do you want me to do?" Elias whispered.

She looked at him for a long moment. Then she reached into her pocket, pulled out a photograph, and handed it to him.

A child. A boy. Eight or nine. Laughing. His eyes matched hers.

"My brother," she said. "He disappeared when I was fifteen. Gone without a trace. But I remember someone had sketched him that morning, near the old train station. He said a man had drawn his face in colors. I didn't understand then. But now..."

She exhaled. "I think he was one of yours."

"No," Elias said. "I wasn't even here ten years ago. I didn't even start drawing like this until I was in my twenties."

She stared at him.

And then her face changed. Something in it collapsed—not into sadness, but into something deeper. A tired understanding.

"Then it's not just you," she said softly. "You're not the first."

By: Alden Blake

She backed away, still looking at the sketch on the ground.

"I just wanted to see," she said. "If I let you draw me, would I disappear too? Would I find out where they all went?"

Elias stood now. "You're not going to vanish," he said. "It doesn't work like that."

She smiled. For the first time. It wasn't a joyful smile.

"I hope not," she said. "But I also hope I do."

And she turned and walked away.

He didn't draw again for days.

―――――――――――――――――――――――

But the silence didn't last.

That Friday, he returned to a narrow plaza near the river, hoping to feel normal again. He planned to sketch only the landscape. Just bricks, railings, water. Nothing human.

And then he saw her again.

The woman.

She stood across the street, hands in her coat pockets, watching him. Not smiling. Not moving.

He stared.

And then someone stepped in front of his view—an elderly man with a cane. Elias blinked.

When the man passed, she was gone.

He ran across. Checked the sidewalks, the alleyways. Nothing. No trace. Not even footprints.

When he returned to his mat, something was wrong.

There, on the pavement where he'd left only colorless marks, was a drawing.

Her face. Finished.

But he hadn't drawn it.

It was done in a softer hand. Lines thinner. More deliberate. More intimate.

The chalk that formed her mouth had begun to smear, as if she were already fading.

That night, Elias couldn't eat. Couldn't sleep. He paced the floor of his apartment, surrounded by the ghost gallery of all he'd ever drawn. The question grew louder inside him.

Was this a gift—or a curse?

What if he wasn't *stealing* people—but catching something they were trying to leave behind? A last breath. A moment of surrender. A secret wish to vanish.

What if the chalk didn't create the disappearance—but gave it permission?

He thought of her last words: *"I hope I do."*

And then he wept.

For the first time in years.

In the weeks that followed, Elias tried something new.

He asked.

Every time he drew someone, he stopped them first.

"Can I draw you?" he'd say. "Just a sketch. Just for a moment."

Most said no.

A few said yes.

And none of them vanished.

Until one did.

An old woman with silver braids and a cracked smile. She'd said yes, then sat beside him while he worked. They talked about music. About her granddaughter. About the smell of bread on winter mornings.

And then she stood, thanked him, and walked into the square.

She passed behind the fountain.

And never came out the other side.

Elias sat there for hours, waiting.

He never saw her again.

Only the chalk on his hands. And a sketch, drying in the sun. Her smile just beginning to smudge.

He doesn't draw every day now. And when he does, it's not for beauty. Or for art.

It's for something else.

A kind of remembering. A quiet sending off.

He doesn't know where they go. Or why.

But when he finishes a portrait, he sometimes sees something shimmer at the edge of his vision. Like a door opening, too quickly to step through.

And sometimes—just sometimes—he hears a voice, faint and far:

Thank you.

By: Alden Blake

He doesn't know if it's real.

But he keeps drawing. Just in case.

There were days now when Elias would sit among the smudged remains of chalk drawings, half-faded in the sun, and wonder if he existed at all.

He'd stopped trying to keep track. Of the people. Of the count. Of the reasons.

He knew that when he drew someone with real care—when his fingers moved as if remembering rather than creating—something *happened*. Not every time, but often enough that the mystery had taken on the weight of a law. Not logic, but inevitability.

Some vanished entirely. Others, it seemed, simply *changed*. They'd look different the next time he saw them—older or younger, lighter or heavier, as if the chalk had altered their density in the world.

One man had walked up to him two weeks after a portrait and said, in a voice soft with awe, "I saw myself in a dream last night. Not as I am now. As I was when I first believed I'd be happy. It was the same face you drew."

He had tears in his eyes.

"I don't know what that means," the man added.

Neither did Elias.

And yet he kept going back.

There was no answer in the drawings themselves. He tried analyzing them—looking for patterns, missing lines, symbolic shadows. But they were just portraits. Sincere, sometimes beautiful. Always ordinary.

Until they weren't.

One morning, Elias sat in the middle of the empty Roten Square, surrounded by his supplies, with no intention of drawing. He stared at the stone fountain, cracked and dry, and felt the strange pressure of absence. The kind that came before a choice.

A girl approached him. Maybe twelve. Alone. Barefoot.

He flinched when he saw her, as if he knew her.

"I dreamed of you," she said without smiling.

"Did you?"

She nodded. "You were drawing birds, but they didn't have wings."

"What else did you see?"

"You were crying," she said. "And the sky was the color of paper. Not blue. Just... paper."

He stared at her.

By: Alden Blake

She sat beside him, cross-legged, and said, "Can you draw me now?"

"No," he said.

"Why not?"

"Because I think it's dangerous."

She smiled faintly. "So is remembering."

He wanted to argue. But she reached into her coat and pulled out a small, folded paper crane. "If I vanish," she said, "keep this."

Elias stared at the origami.

"What if you don't come back?" he whispered.

"Then I went where the birds go," she said. "The ones with no wings."

She stayed still while he drew. Perfectly still. Her eyes closed. As if she were already somewhere else.

When he finished, the chalk in his hands had worn to dust. The likeness on the pavement shimmered faintly in the morning light. And she was gone.

No footstep. No rustle. Not even a sigh.

He touched the crane. It was real. Still warm.

Elias kept it.

Years passed.

He drew fewer portraits. He took to sketching silence instead—abandoned chairs, doorways left ajar, lamplight pooling on brick walls. Things that could neither vanish nor explain themselves.

But the people kept coming.

Some sat without asking.

Some whispered names before he began.

Some left him notes: *Don't be afraid. I'm ready.*

He didn't know what they were ready for. Or who they believed he was.

All he knew was this: each drawing felt like a threshold. As if the world had bent slightly to let something through—or out.

One night, he stood before a mirror and tried to draw himself.

He couldn't do it.

The lines wouldn't hold.

By: Alden Blake

His hand trembled. The chalk broke. Again and again.

In the end, he drew a blank face. Featureless. Waiting.

He didn't vanish.

Not then.

There was an old philosopher he once read who claimed that art wasn't about expressing anything— but about *releasing* something we can't otherwise name. Elias wondered, now, if his chalk had been naming people too clearly.

Maybe the drawings made their subjects too *true*—like lanterns revealing what the world had chosen to blur.

And once someone became that real, maybe they no longer belonged here.

Maybe they belonged *somewhere else*.

He dreamed often, now.

In one dream, he was in a gallery where all the paintings were mirrors.

In another, he saw the paper city he'd once imagined as a child, only this time it was full of people—smiling, waving, and made entirely of linework and light.

Sometimes, he dreamed of the girl with the crane.

She was older now. Or perhaps he was younger.

They were drawing each other in the same sketchbook, page after page, until the book disappeared in their hands.

On a quiet morning in late autumn, Elias walked to the riverbank. Not to draw. Just to sit.

A little boy ran past, chasing a feather caught on the wind.

Elias closed his eyes.

When he opened them, the chalk was in his hand again.

He didn't remember picking it up.

He looked down.

The pavement beside him was blank. Clean.

A canvas.

For what?

He began to draw—not a face, not a body. Just movement. Just the memory of hands reaching

By: Alden Blake

toward something just beyond the page. The curve of laughter. The edge of a name.

And then the girl's crane fluttered from his coat pocket and landed on the drawing.

No wind.

Just descent.

It glowed for a moment, then stilled.

Elias sat back.

The line was done.

He waited.

No one vanished.

Nothing shimmered.

But somewhere, very faintly, he heard a sound he hadn't heard in a long time:

Laughter.

Soft. Real.

And completely unfamiliar.

It came from nowhere and everywhere—like a memory that wasn't his, but had always been waiting to be heard.

He looked around. No one was there.

But the sound remained, echoing just at the edge of hearing.

Not haunting.

Not cruel.

Just... human.

He smiled.

And for the first time, he wondered if the sketches weren't about disappearing at all.

Maybe they were about finding a way back.

Not to this world—but to whatever waits behind the veil of what we choose to see.

A return not to place—but to meaning.

To the truth of being seen—and drawn—fully.

When they found Elias years later, his chalks had long since worn down to stubs. He had no family. No known history. Just a street corner stained with faint outlines—hundreds of them—some fading into cobblestone, some still crisp. A portfolio full of names he never knew.

And a single paper crane.

Unfolded.

Inside, in faded graphite, was a single line:

"We are not made to last—only to be glimpsed."

No one ever claimed the body.

But from time to time, someone would visit the square, kneel beside a drawing, and whisper a name.

And sometimes—just sometimes—they'd smile.

As if someone had answered.

Chapter 6:

Where the Dandelions Grow

The house stood just as they'd left it, and nothing like it at all.

Ivy had conquered the porch steps. The roof sagged slightly under the weight of time. Windowpanes were clouded with dust, like cataracts in a sleeping giant's eyes. The once-white paint had faded to a hue somewhere between smoke and memory.

Caleb stood with the key in his hand and hesitation in his posture.

"It looks smaller," he said.

By: Alden Blake

Mira adjusted the backpack on her shoulder, squinting toward the overgrown garden. "Everything does when you're taller."

They hadn't been here in fifteen years. Not since the funeral. Not since the lawyer handed them a will written in their mother's delicate cursive, requesting—no, insisting—they let the house rest for a while. Let it breathe. And when the time felt right, come back together.

"Right," Caleb muttered, finally fitting the key into the lock. "As if houses breathe."

But the door sighed open.

And the air inside was the same: a mixture of cedar, dust, and something softer—like sugar cookies, or lilacs. Something invisible but familiar.

They stepped in together.

The boards creaked beneath their feet like an old voice murmuring its first words after a long silence.

The house wasn't untouched. Nature had crept in at the corners—moss on the windowsills, tiny tendrils of vine curling along the kitchen sink, where a spider had claimed dominion over the faucet. But it wasn't ruined. It was resting. Exactly as their mother had wanted.

They explored in silence at first. Mira traced her fingers along the wallpaper, its faded pattern of vines and moons. Caleb ran his hand along the banister they'd once slid down as children.

The upstairs hallway was still lined with picture frames. Family photos. A watercolor painting of the garden. And that odd charcoal sketch of a dandelion field their mother had insisted was "based on something real," though neither of them ever remembered seeing such a place.

In the guest room, Caleb found a box labeled "TO BE OPENED BY THEM, TOGETHER."

Mira sat beside him on the floor as he lifted the lid.

Inside: an old Polaroid of the two of them in the garden, faces smudged with dirt and grinning wildly; a letter in their mother's handwriting; and a small cloth pouch filled with dandelion seeds.

The letter read:

> *To my wildflowers,*
>
> *If you're reading this, you've returned.*
> *That means the time is right.*
> *You were always chasing pieces of the past—trying to catch it in your hands like fireflies.*
> *But the garden remembers what you*

forget. Especially what's buried beneath it.

Go where the dandelions grow.

Love always,
 Mama

Mira looked up. "She's talking about the garden."

Caleb nodded. "Or what's left of it."

They stood and walked out the back door.

The garden had become a wilderness.

Dandelions ruled now—gold-headed, defiant, unbothered by the years. They spilled across the grass like stars fallen from the sky. Tall weeds swayed lazily in the breeze. The old stone path was nearly swallowed, a cracked serpent of granite leading nowhere and everywhere.

"She used to say dandelions were weeds that dreamed of being flowers," Mira said.

"And we believed her."

They walked slowly, letting memory guide them. Here was where the tire swing used to hang. There was the stump where Caleb once hammered bottle caps into a smiley face. The fountain, long dry. The rose bushes—

withered, skeletal, yet still guarding their thorny perimeter.

In the center of the garden was something unexpected: a circle of dandelions more vibrant than the rest, glowing faintly in the afternoon sun.

It was too perfect to be natural.

Mira stepped into the circle. "This is where we buried it."

Caleb froze. "Buried what?"

She didn't answer at first. Instead, she knelt and ran her fingers through the dirt. "You don't remember?"

He shook his head, slowly. "No."

But something fluttered behind his eyes. A moment. A shadow. A whisper.

"We buried something," Mira said softly. "Something Mama told us to forget."

Caleb felt a strange pressure in his chest. Not pain. More like the weight of recognition.

A secret returning.

Mira stood and handed him the pouch of seeds.

"We should plant them here," she said.

By: Alden Blake

Caleb didn't ask why. He knelt beside her, cleared a small patch in the center of the circle, and together they pressed the seeds into the earth.

As they worked, the wind picked up. Soft. Almost songlike.

And in that moment, as the dandelions danced, the house behind them seemed to exhale.

A long, patient breath.

Waiting. Watching.

Remembering.

By the time the sun slipped behind the old poplars, the dandelions had begun to glow.

It wasn't the light of reflection or the faint shimmer of dew—it was something subtler. A quiet luminescence, as if the memory of sunlight lingered longer in this part of the garden than the rest of the world allowed. Mira sat cross-legged in the grass, watching them breathe.

"They're brighter here," she said.

Caleb didn't answer. He was kneeling at the edge of the dandelion circle, pulling away the encroaching weeds. His hands were dirty. His brow was furrowed in that particular way Mira hadn't seen since their mother's diagnosis—an expression caught between resistance and revelation.

"I remember the song," he said suddenly.

"What song?"

"She used to sing it when we'd lie in the grass." He didn't look up. "The one about the golden field and the lion asleep in the flowers."

Mira's voice came out softer than she intended. "You were four."

"I didn't remember it until now."

They sat in silence, the last birdsong curling like smoke above them. The house behind them creaked in the settling dusk.

Mira spoke first. "Do you remember what happened after the funeral?"

He nodded, slowly. "I remember that we left. Fast. Without packing anything."

"And you stopped talking for three weeks."

"I didn't know that."

"You wouldn't," she said, brushing dandelion fluff from her knee. "You never saw it."

He looked at her then—really looked. Her eyes were wet, but steady. "What do you mean?"

"You didn't cry, Caleb. Not even once. You just... closed."

By: Alden Blake

Inside the house, the hallway still smelled faintly of cinnamon and mothballs. Mira lit a candle, its wick reluctant. They moved room by room, saying little, touching familiar things like archaeologists uncovering the ruins of childhood.

In the linen closet, Mira found her old stuffed fox, one button eye missing.

In the attic, Caleb uncovered the wooden puzzle box they used to hide coins in—still locked, still heavy.

In the kitchen, the fridge bore a brittle paper magnet with the word *HOPE* curled at its edges.

They paused at the bottom of the stairs.

"I remember the night we got snowed in," Mira said. "We couldn't sleep, so Mom made us pancakes at midnight."

"And told us the story of the dandelion king," Caleb added.

Mira smiled. "The one who wore a crown of seeds and only spoke in riddles."

Caleb stepped away and leaned against the banister. His voice turned quieter. "Do you think she knew she was sick then?"

Mira hesitated. "Maybe. She always knew things before we did."

Caleb looked at the living room, at the cold fireplace and dust-veiled windows. "We're walking around this house like it's a museum."

"It kind of is."

"Or a mausoleum."

They returned to the garden by moonlight.

The dandelion circle was glowing brighter now, almost pulsing—faint, golden breaths.

"We buried something here," Mira whispered.

"Or someone."

She turned to him sharply.

"I don't mean that literally," he said. "I just... what if this isn't a place we left behind—but something that was hiding in us this whole time?"

She crouched and began to dig—not deeply, just brushing the soil aside with her fingers. Caleb joined her.

The earth was soft. Willing.

In minutes, they hit something hard.

By: Alden Blake

Wood.

A small, weathered box—no bigger than a lunch tin. Mira lifted it free with trembling hands.

The lid opened with a reluctant creak.

Inside: a crumpled piece of drawing paper. A bracelet made of twine and plastic beads. A photograph of the three of them—Mira, Caleb, and their mother— standing beneath a willow tree, grinning through smudges of dirt. And a note.

Mira unfolded it.

Her mother's handwriting was shakier here, rushed.

> *You were too young to carry this when it happened.*
> *I asked you to forget. And you did.*
> *But memories buried too deep start to grow strange roots.*
>
> *You'll feel them again, now. It's okay.*
> *You're older.*
>
> *The dandelions will help you remember— but gently.*
>
> *Just don't run this time.*
>
> *Love,*
> *Mama*

Caleb took the bracelet in his hand. "I made this."

"You gave it to her," Mira said. "After the hospital."

Caleb nodded slowly, remembering something not with words, but with the weight in his chest. "She gave it back before the funeral."

"She said it should go in the box."

They stared at the note.

Neither wanted to speak the question aloud, but it lived between them:
 What are we supposed to remember now?

Later that night, Mira couldn't sleep. She returned to the garden alone.

The dandelions swayed even without wind. She lay among them and closed her eyes.

And in that strange, hushed dark—just before sleep— she remembered.

The argument.

Her mother, hunched over a letter.

Mira screaming. Caleb crying in the hallway.

The truth spilled in fragments—terminal, months, not enough time.

By: Alden Blake

She remembered her mother kneeling in the garden that last week, planting the seeds with trembling hands, telling them stories with a voice cracked by morphine and hope.

Telling them:
One day, this will bloom into a memory worth returning to.

When she returned to the house, Caleb was sitting on the stairs.

"I remember too," he said.

"Tell me."

He didn't. Instead, he reached into his pocket and pulled out something new: a crumpled sketch.

A child's drawing. The three of them, smiling, surrounded by yellow flowers.

"It was under my pillow," he said. "Like it was waiting."

Mira stared at it for a long moment. Then she smiled.

"Maybe the house does breathe," she said.

"Maybe it dreams."

The next morning was thick with mist. The sky had not yet decided if it would be blue or gray, and the air held that in-between quiet reserved for old forests and childhood homes. Mira stood at the back door, cradling a mug of lukewarm coffee, watching the dandelions bend under the slow breath of morning.

Caleb joined her, wordless, the old drawing still in his pocket. Neither had said much since the night before. There was a weight between them, not heavy with dread, but with a hush—as if something sacred had been remembered.

"What do you think she meant," Mira finally said, "about memories growing strange roots?"

Caleb shrugged, gently. "Maybe that they change shape underground. That if we bury something too long, we forget what it was—but not that it mattered."

They walked into the garden again, side by side. The circle of dandelions was brighter than ever, glowing gold even in the morning gray. Mira knelt where the box had been. She pressed her palm to the soil.

"There's something else," she said.

"How do you know?"

"I don't," she whispered. "But I do."

Caleb fetched a rusted trowel from the shed. Together, they began to dig. Carefully. Slowly. Like they were excavating not just dirt, but time.

By: Alden Blake

In the earth beneath the dandelions, they unearthed a second box—larger, older. Covered in waxed cloth and wrapped in string. Mold had crept across its corners, but it was intact.

Mira stared at it for a long time before lifting it free.

"What is it?" Caleb asked.

"A memory," she said, though she hadn't opened it yet.

When she did, the scent of cedar and dried herbs rose from within, layered with the dusty perfume of the past. Inside lay a single item: a crown.

Not a royal crown, but a handmade one—woven of twigs and dried dandelions, now delicate with age. Tiny feathers and beads were laced into it, and around the inner rim, written in her mother's unmistakable script, were the words:

For the one who remembers gladness.

Mira touched it reverently, as if it might vanish beneath her fingers.

"I remember this," she said. "We made it one summer. She called me her little empress of sunshine. Said every garden needed a ruler."

Caleb smiled. "You wore it for days. Even to bed."

"I cried when the dandelions fell apart."

"I cried when you made me wear it after."

They both laughed softly—an old, round laughter, not quite joy, not quite sorrow, but something in between. Something human.

"I think she meant for us to find it now," Caleb said. "Not then. Not when it was just play."

"Now that we know what it means."

Mira lifted the crown. It felt impossibly light. She placed it gently on the ground between them.

"It's not just about nostalgia," she said. "It's about healing. About remembering that joy once lived here. That it still can."

Caleb nodded. "Even if it's a different kind."

They spent the rest of the day tending the garden. Pulling weeds, clearing old paths, trimming back wild vines. They didn't talk much, but the silence felt companionable—filled with the echoes of stories they no longer had to retell.

At one point, Caleb found the old wind chime that had once hung by the porch. The string was brittle, the metal tarnished. He cleaned it gently, then hung it from a low branch near the dandelion circle.

By: Alden Blake

The first breeze that touched it let out a sound like a sigh being remembered.

That night, they built a small fire in the pit their mother had left behind. Mira brought out marshmallows—somehow still soft from the old pantry—and Caleb found a forgotten guitar, its strings slightly out of tune.

They didn't speak of what came next. Whether to sell the house or keep it. Whether to return to their lives or start something new.

Some questions didn't need immediate answers.

Instead, they sat by the fire, watching embers drift into the night like red-tipped memories.

When the time came to leave, a week later, they stood at the edge of the garden.

The dandelions had begun to go to seed.

Tufts of white shimmered in the breeze, the flowers giving up their golden crowns for a different kind of glory—one that floated, fragile and free.

Mira turned to Caleb, the crown in her hands. "Do you want to take it?"

He shook his head. "It belongs here."

So she knelt, cleared a small place in the soil, and buried the crown again—this time with intention.

A seed planted, not a secret hidden.

"Goodbye," she said softly.

"See you soon," Caleb added.

They didn't lock the door when they left. Just closed it gently.

Years later, a new family would buy the house.

They'd find the garden strange at first, overgrown with dandelions that bloomed longer than they should. Their daughter would spend hours lying among them, humming songs she never learned.

She'd claim she saw two shadows in the mist—one with a crown, one with a drawing in his pocket.

And when asked what she meant, she'd only smile.

"Old kings," she'd say. "They're not sad. Just waiting."

Reflection

Joy doesn't return all at once. It drips back in—like sunlight through shutters, like a melody remembered

By: Alden Blake

in fragments. Nostalgia isn't just longing; it's the bridge we build to cross the dark water of grief.

And healing?

Healing is digging in the soil of memory—not to uproot, but to make space. To breathe. To remember that what was once loved is never truly lost.

In the place where the dandelions grow, things do not vanish.

They transform.

CHAPTER 7:
THE HOURGLASS COLLECTOR

In the city of Chronis, time was not measured by clocks or calendars but by the fragile sands held within countless hourglasses that lined the shelves of every shop and stall. The city's heartbeat pulsed to the rhythm of shifting sands, each grain a fragment of someone's life — bought, sold, borrowed, or stolen.

Morning mist curled between the narrow streets, weaving through crooked towers and crooked alleys. The air smelled faintly of old parchment, burnt candlewax, and something intangible — the weight of moments lost and found. Above the marketplace, colorful banners fluttered in the breeze, painted with symbols of sand, stars, and spirals that seemed to shift if you looked too long.

By: Alden Blake

In a small, dimly lit shop tucked beneath a leaning stone building, a bell chimed softly as the door opened.

Inside, rows upon rows of hourglasses gleamed under the flickering light of oil lamps. Some were tiny, no bigger than a walnut, their sands shimmering like crushed gemstones; others towered nearly a foot high, ornate and delicate, their frames carved with ancient runes.

At the center of this glass menagerie stood a man — tall and slender, with eyes the color of storm clouds and hands weathered from years of careful handling. He was the Hourglass Collector.

His name was Aelor.

Aelor had spent decades in Chronis, trading time for coin, piecing together moments that others discarded or feared to spend. His shop was filled not only with hourglasses but with stories — whispers of laughter, tears, whispered promises, and forgotten dreams, all trapped inside the delicate vessels.

Though surrounded by countless fragments of other lives, Aelor was lonely. The weight of time had a way of isolating him, a reminder that every grain slipping through the glass was a moment he could never reclaim for himself.

Yet, each day, he welcomed those who sought his wares — travelers chasing youth, lovers hoping to stretch a stolen hour, dreamers longing to buy a second chance.

Today, as the sun barely pierced through the gray clouds, Aelor polished a small hourglass filled with golden sand — sand he called the "Hour of Gladness," a time said to have disappeared from the city centuries ago. Many believed it was a myth, a tale told to children to give hope. But Aelor had spent years searching, convinced that if he could find this lost hour, he could unlock a secret buried deep within the flow of time itself.

His fingers traced the glass carefully, feeling the warmth of the sand as it trickled slowly from the top chamber to the bottom.

The door creaked open again, and a young woman stepped inside, her eyes wide with wonder and fatigue.

"Are you the Collector?" she asked.

Aelor nodded, his voice soft as the ticking of a distant clock. "I am. What time do you seek?"

She hesitated, then whispered, "An hour that never runs out."

Aelor sat behind his worn wooden counter, the weight of twilight settling over Chronis like a slow sigh. The flickering oil lamps cast dancing shadows across the shelves, making the hourglasses shimmer as if they

By: Alden Blake

held tiny stars trapped inside. But tonight, even their soft glow couldn't brighten the heaviness in his chest.

He cradled a delicate hourglass in his hands — its sands pale gold, flowing slowly through the narrow waist. This was not just any hourglass. This was a shard of legend, a sliver of time whispered about in hushed tones among traders and dreamers: the Hour of Gladness.

For years, Aelor had hunted for it, chasing fragments of rumors that slipped through the city like fine dust. Some said the Hour of Gladness was a lost moment, stolen from the world in some forgotten tragedy; others claimed it was a gift, a secret blessing that vanished once the city lost its innocence.

But no one had seen it—until Aelor began collecting stories, piecing together shards from old journals, faded maps, and conversations overheard in smoky taverns.

He fingered the hourglass again, watching the grains fall like melted sunlight. If he could find the full hour—an unbroken stretch of pure joy, untouched by sorrow—he believed it could change everything. Maybe even mend the invisible fractures running through the city's soul.

Yet every search deepened the melancholy within him. Time, after all, was a cruel master. The more he sought, the more he realized that joy was not a thing to hold onto but a fragile, fleeting spark—one that slipped away no matter how tightly he tried to grasp it.

His thoughts were interrupted by a soft knock on the door.

Aelor looked up to see an old man leaning on a cane, his eyes sharp beneath heavy brows.

"Looking for something rare, Collector?" the man asked, voice gravelly but calm.

Aelor nodded slowly. "The Hour of Gladness."

The old man chuckled, a dry sound like leaves rustling in autumn. "Many chase what cannot be caught. That hour was lost when the city first sold its first grief."

"Tell me," Aelor said, voice barely a whisper. "Where was it last seen?"

The man's eyes flickered with a distant memory. "By the river, before the great flood. They say it slipped through the cracks of a broken hourglass, swallowed by the current and carried into the depths where time bends."

Aelor's heart tightened. The river had been a place of childhood laughter and sorrow for him—now just a shadowed memory.

"Why do you seek it?" the old man asked, stepping closer.

By: Alden Blake

"To find something worth holding onto," Aelor replied. "To remember that happiness once lived here."

The old man nodded slowly. "Be careful, Collector. Sometimes the past doesn't want to be found."

As the door closed behind the visitor, Aelor felt the ache of his solitary quest deepen. The hourglass glowed faintly in his hands — a reminder that even the brightest moments must eventually fall through.

And so, beneath the city's endless ticking, the Collector prepared to follow the river's ghost—into the place where lost time waited, silent and waiting to be found.

The sky over Chronis was bruised with clouds, and a soft rain began to fall as Aelor made his way to the river—the place the old man had spoken of. The streets were slick with wet cobblestones, and the distant murmur of water mingled with the city's steady pulse. The river cut like a silver ribbon through the heart of Chronis, its current both a boundary and a pathway to forgotten things.

Aelor carried a small satchel filled with tools— magnifying glasses, tiny brushes, and several empty hourglasses. His fingers traced the worn leather as he walked, thinking of the tales of the lost Hour of Gladness. Was it really gone? Or had it simply changed form, hiding in a place no one dared look?

He reached the riverbank just as the rain softened to a mist. The water moved quietly, swirling past old stone steps that had once led down to a bustling quay now swallowed by weeds and silence.

Kneeling, Aelor ran his fingers through the cold mud, searching for anything that might hint at the past. Hours passed in near darkness as he sifted through detritus: shattered glass, rusted coins, a child's broken toy. Nothing that gleamed like the golden sands he sought.

As night crept over the city, Aelor felt the weight of failure pressing down on him. The Hour of Gladness remained elusive, a phantom slipping through his grasp like so many grains of sand.

He pulled out an empty hourglass from his bag and sat back against a stone pillar. Quietly, he turned it upside down and watched as the clear sand began to fall.

And then, a thought settled in his mind—one he hadn't fully admitted before.

Perhaps the Hour of Gladness was never meant to be captured. Perhaps it was not a prize hidden beneath the river or buried in the city's history, but something that lived only in the longing itself.

The longing to remember joy, to hold onto it, even when it vanished.

By: Alden Blake

Aelor sat by the river, the hourglass running empty, and slowly began to fill the bottom chamber with sand he collected from the riverbank. Each grain was imperfect, worn smooth by time and water, yet together they formed a new measure—a fragile, hopeful timepiece.

He realized then that the value was not in possessing a perfect hour but in cherishing the search, the hope, the aching desire for something more.

The next morning, Aelor returned to his shop, the river's mist clinging to his coat. He placed the new hourglass on the shelf—not as a treasure, but as a symbol. A reminder that sometimes, what we chase isn't a moment frozen in glass, but the very feeling of longing that makes life worth living.

And in the quiet city of Chronis, where time was always slipping away, that was perhaps the greatest gift of all.

Reflection

The Hourglass Collector never found the lost hour he sought. Instead, he discovered that longing itself was a kind of time—an endless flow that connected past and future, joy and sorrow, loss and hope.

Because some moments are not meant to be held.

They are meant to be remembered.

And in remembering, we live again.

CHAPTER 8:
THE TRAIN TO NO YESTERDAY

It was said the train never stopped—not for stations, not for storms, not even for sleep. It carved its way across a vast and nameless landscape, its tracks swallowed by fog on either end. There were no conductors, no visible engineers. Just the low hum of the wheels against metal and the persistent whisper of wind slipping through the cracks.

No one remembered boarding.
No one remembered where they were going.

The passengers existed in a kind of soft blur, like dreams held too long. They moved through the cars in quiet loops, touching door frames as if for reassurance, murmuring names they no longer trusted to be theirs. Some had been on the train for days. Others claimed it had been years. Time didn't count the same aboard the Train to No Yesterday.

The seats were mismatched—wooden benches from old city trams, plush velvet armchairs, plastic commuter seats bolted to the floor. The light flickered between dawn and dusk, never quite deciding whether it was morning or night.

Some passengers looked out the windows, though the view offered little. Fields gave way to oceans, then to cities made entirely of scaffolding and birds. There were mountains with windows in their cliffs, and deserts where shadows moved ahead of the sun. No matter how long one watched, the scenery never repeated—but it never clarified either.

At the back of Car Seven sat a man in a green wool coat, his face half-shadowed by the brim of a hat that didn't seem to fit quite right. A battered suitcase rested beside him, its corners soft with age, its latch tied shut with twine. He had a notebook open in his lap. A pencil hovered over the page.

He wasn't sure of his name.

Sometimes it came to him in a flash—"Arthur," maybe, or "Samir," or once, quite vividly, "Lachlan." But the feeling never lasted. Like the images outside the window, it slipped away before he could hold it.

What he did know was this: he had to remember. Not everything—just the joy.

By: Alden Blake

It had been a color, once. A voice, a scent. A pair of hands holding his. A laugh that cracked open the ordinary and let in something light. He couldn't recall the shape of it, but he knew it had been real.

So he wrote.

Each morning—or whatever passed for morning on the train—he tore a page from his notebook and scrawled a message. He kept the words simple, afraid complexity might dissolve in the ether like everything else.

> "You used to love music."
> "There was a tree you climbed every summer."
> "Someone waited for you in the rain."

He signed each with whatever name felt closest to true. Then he slipped the paper into a blank postcard, addressed it to himself—no city, no street, just a name—and dropped it into the slit of an old mailbox bolted to the wall near the dining car. It wasn't always there, the mailbox. Some mornings it vanished. Some mornings it bled rust. But the man in the green coat never missed a chance when it appeared.

He didn't expect to receive the postcards back. But writing them kept the thread taut. If memory was a wall collapsing inward, the postcards were stones he tossed into the void, hoping one might hit bottom.

He wasn't alone in this ritual. Other passengers had their own methods.

An elderly woman in Car Two carved initials into the window with a pocketknife. A boy no older than twelve whispered apologies into a broken walkie-talkie. A former teacher, judging by the chalk dust on her sleeves, ran spelling drills in the aisles, though no one answered.

Each person gripped a fragment of the past, worn down to splinters.

One day, while pressing his postcard into the slot, the man noticed something strange—another card already half-inserted. He pulled it out. The front was blank. No image, no stamp. But on the back, written in looping, careful script:

> "You were looking for something beautiful. Don't stop."

There was no signature. No return address. He looked around, but the hallway was empty.

The next morning, another message appeared.

> "Do you remember the melody? It hummed from your coat pocket."

He held the card for a long time. A melody. Yes—there had been music, hadn't there? Not something grand. Something small, intimate. A music box? A hum in someone's throat? He couldn't place it. But when he closed his eyes, he could almost hear it—the outline of a tune, the ghost of rhythm.

The postcards kept coming.

Each one was placed exactly where he would find it: beneath his coffee cup, tucked into his coat sleeve, balanced on the rim of the sink in the washroom. Always typed or handwritten. Always addressed to him—by implication, if not by name.

> "There was a garden. You planted mint
> and forgot the basil."
> "Your father's hands smelled like engine
> grease and oranges."
> "She danced with bare feet in the snow."

The details grew sharper. More personal. Not just the past, but *his* past. Whoever wrote them knew things he didn't remember until he read them.

One night—he called it night because the stars outside pulsed rather than moved—he found a folded note taped to the window beside his seat.

> "Go to Car Eleven."

He hadn't dared pass Car Ten before. Beyond that, the train changed. Passengers said it got... *strange*. The rhythm of the wheels altered. Lights flickered blue instead of yellow. The air felt thick, like being underwater.

But curiosity pulled him forward.

He passed through empty cars, some dimly lit, others nearly pitch black. Car Nine smelled of lilacs and rust. Car Ten had a piano that played itself, keys moving without sound. When he reached Car Eleven, he hesitated.

The door slid open on its own.

Inside was a library.

Thousands of books, stacked floor to ceiling, none labeled. No librarian. No system. The smell of paper was overwhelming—warm, dusty, alive. He stepped inside and immediately noticed something strange: the titles were changing.

As he pulled a book from the shelf, the title on the spine shifted beneath his fingers.

> *The House with No Walls*
> *All the Places You Never Looked*
> *Gladness, Once*

The final one froze him.

He opened it. The pages were blank, save for a single sentence written in the middle of the book:

"You have been here before."

He closed the book. Sat on the nearest bench. And for the first time since he had awoken on the train, he wept.

By: Alden Blake

It wasn't sadness. It wasn't fear. It was recognition. Not of the room, or the train, or even himself—but of a feeling. A warmth. A flicker of color that hadn't yet gone out.

Joy.

It had lived here once. In this place. In him.

And maybe, just maybe, it wasn't entirely gone.

He called himself many names—Cal, Jonas, Eli, once even Harold—but none of them stuck long. The train had a way of eroding certainty. Still, the act of naming gave him shape, like drawing an outline in the fog. Today, he signed the postcard "Théo." He didn't know why. The name just felt like someone who might have loved to laugh.

The postcard was plain. Cream-colored, slightly curled at the edges. He scrawled the date—though he had no idea what it was—and then paused.

What had he remembered?

Sometimes the memories came as impressions. A color that made his breath hitch. A sound that rang strangely familiar. A scent—rosemary and rain, perhaps—that made his fingers tremble with the urge to hold something, or someone, now gone.

He wrote:

"You once woke up to the sound of birds in
an unfamiliar city and knew—just knew—
that you were finally free."

He read the sentence three times before folding it into
the card. It didn't matter if it was true. The memory
had *felt* real in the moment it appeared, and that was
enough.

The mailbox was gone today, of course. It disappeared
without pattern. But that didn't stop him. He tucked
the postcard into the breast pocket of his green coat,
buttoned it shut, and whispered aloud: "Don't forget.
Please, don't forget."

The train slid on, silent as a thought. In Car Seven, a
man played chess against himself with mismatched
pieces. In Car Three, a young woman sewed buttons
onto a map. No one looked at each other for too long.
Eyes were dangerous here—mirrors of recognition, or
worse, forgetfulness.

That afternoon—though time felt like a dream here—
Théo sat by the window and tried to conjure the sound
of laughter. Not any laughter. *Her* laughter. Whoever
she had been.

He could almost hear it: a staccato rhythm, light at
first, then full-bodied, rising like a flame. She had
laughed at something he'd said, he was certain. Not a
joke—he wasn't that clever—but something accidental.
A comment about the color of clouds, maybe, or how
spoons never felt cold enough.

By: Alden Blake

He opened his notebook and wrote:

> "Her laughter made the walls brighter.
> Even the wallpaper leaned in to listen."

That one he didn't mail. He tore it out and tucked it between the pages of a book he kept in his suitcase—a copy of *Siddhartha* he didn't remember owning but always carried.

It was how he kept his archive.

Most passengers had their rituals. He'd seen a man fold paper cranes out of napkins, one for every word he remembered. A woman embroidered dates into the lining of her dress. A boy scribbled in the margins of a tattered comic book, muttering words that sounded like poems.

But Théo had the postcards. Dozens of them, stored in the case under his seat. Some were hopeful:

> "You danced once, in a kitchen, with flour
> on your hands."

Others were aching:

> "You watched someone walk away without
> saying goodbye. You never learned why."

And a few were simply strange:

> "The red umbrella wasn't yours, but it felt
> like it should be."

They weren't always about joy, strictly speaking. But they circled it. Mapped its absence, its memory, its echo. That was the point. He wasn't trying to find happiness. He was trying to prove it had ever existed at all.

Somewhere in the train—perhaps Car Eleven, or maybe farther still—was a girl who sang to herself in a language no one recognized. One night, he had passed her car and paused outside the sliding door, just to listen. Her voice had curled around the melody like smoke. He didn't know the words, but they stirred something.

The next day, he wrote:

> "You understood a language once. Not
> with words, but with feeling."

He'd wanted to give it to her, to slip it into her hand without explanation. But he hadn't dared. People on the train didn't often touch. Contact felt... risky. As though too much intimacy might pull someone out of their loop—or worse, erase what little they still remembered.

So he kept it in the case, like all the others.

It had been a long time—if that phrase meant anything here—since he had seen his reflection. Mirrors were rare on the train. When he did catch glimpses—polished silverware, a puddle of spilled tea—he didn't quite recognize the man staring back.

By: Alden Blake

Thin. Eyes tired but alert. A mouth that looked like it had smiled often, even if it didn't lately. The hat he wore was slightly too large. He suspected it hadn't been his originally. But it kept his head warm and gave him the appearance of purpose.

One evening, as the sky outside the windows turned a soft violet, Théo was awoken by a tapping.

He sat up.

There—taped to the glass—was a postcard. Not one of his. The handwriting was too neat.

"What do you miss that you've never had?"

He stared at the card for a long time. That night, he didn't sleep.

The question circled him like a hawk. What *did* he miss that he had never known?

A home with wooden beams and a fireplace that crackled without effort. A daughter with curly hair who called him "Papa." A quiet moment on a pier, watching koi fish ripple the water beside a woman who smelled like honeysuckle.

Were those imagined?

Did it matter?

He wrote back the next day, though he had no way to deliver the reply.

"I miss belonging. I miss being known
without having to be explained."

He tucked it under his pillow, just in case someone—
or something—came looking.

By now, his suitcase was nearly full. Some of the
postcards were dog-eared, ink faded by time or
perhaps the peculiar wear of the train. A few had
begun to feel like fiction. He re-read one:

"Your mother sang while cooking—always
the same song. You never asked what it
meant."

He could no longer hear the tune in his head. But the
act of writing it had once made him cry. That counted
for something.

Occasionally, he wondered if he was the only one still
trying to remember. Others seemed content in their
loops—repeating small rituals, staring into space,
holding tightly to fading tokens. Maybe forgetting was
easier. Cleaner. A kind of mercy.

But Théo wasn't ready to let go. Not yet.

On the next day—again, whatever that meant—the
mailbox returned.

He fed it four cards. Each with a name and a story.
Each a little heavier than the last.

By: Alden Blake

And this time, as he let go of the final one, he whispered not just a plea but a promise:

"I will find you. I will remember."

The mailbox clicked softly, almost kindly, and swallowed the card.

Outside the window, the fog thinned for a moment. Just long enough to reveal a glimpse of a field. A tree. A swing. Someone laughing in the distance.

He pressed his hand to the glass. Closed his eyes.

And smiled.

He dreamed of a station.

Not the kind with clocks or benches, but a station carved from fog and brass, rising out of a sea of shifting sand. It had no name, only a symbol etched above its doors—a circle, cracked down the middle. The sound of the train slowing was strange, like breath being drawn in for the first time.

He stood on the threshold. Others stood beside him. Familiar and not. The woman who sewed buttons into maps. The child with the comic book. The singer from the other car, her mouth full of melody and shadows.

The man in the green coat—Théo, or whatever his name had once been—stepped forward.

And then he woke.

The train had not stopped.

He was still in Car Seven. Still dressed in yesterday's thoughts and tomorrow's name. The dream, like so many things, had faded. But the image of the station lingered, just beyond the curtain of consciousness.

On the seat beside him sat a postcard. Not his own. This one was different—thicker stock, edges gold-leafed. The handwriting was both ornate and familiar.

> "When the train reaches the place that is
> not a place, you may remember who you
> were. Or you may choose who to be. Both
> are forms of truth."

There was no signature. Just a symbol in the corner— a circle, cracked down the middle.

He turned the card over. Blank. But as he stared at it, faint words began to appear, like ink rising through old paper.

> "You once called yourself Julien. You
> wrote a poem about rain that made
> someone fall in love with you."

His breath caught. That name. That memory—it didn't feel like imagination. It felt like the core of something real, long buried. Rain. A poem. A person who had listened, and understood.

He whispered the name: "Julien."

By: Alden Blake

It tasted like a beginning.

And with it came a feeling—not quite joy, but its distant cousin. A warmth behind the ribs. The knowledge that he had, once, meant something to someone.

He left his seat. Walked down the corridor, brushing his hand along the wall as if to stay grounded. The train shifted around him—cars no longer in the order he remembered. Car Eleven came first, then Car Three, then a car made entirely of mirrors.

Inside that mirrored car, he paused.

His reflection stared back—not quite identical. The man in the mirror was him, but *remembered differently*. His coat was darker, his posture straighter. He looked like someone who had loved deeply and lost carefully.

The mirror fogged, and words appeared on the glass:

> "Would you recognize yourself if no one
> else did?"

He reached out. The surface rippled beneath his fingers like water. He stepped through.

Beyond the mirror was a forest.

Yes—a forest, within the train. The trees grew from the floorboards, bark carved with names in dozens of hands. Lanterns hung from the branches, each one glowing with a soft light, each flickering slightly out of sync.

In the clearing stood a man.

He wore a crown. Not gold, not jeweled. Paper. Newsprint, folded and taped. His suit was patchwork—corduroy and linen and things that didn't match. He stood barefoot in the grass, smiling with a kind of tired wonder.

"The Last Emperor of Gladness," Théo—or Julien— said aloud, though he hadn't meant to.

The man nodded. "At least, that's what they call me. But names are soft things here. We are mostly made of our echoes."

Julien stepped forward. "What *are* you?"

The emperor's smile widened just slightly. "I'm a memory you're allowed to keep. Not because I'm important, but because you chose me."

Julien felt something shift inside him. A tether tightening. A weight lifting.

"But why me?" he asked.

The Emperor shrugged. "Because you refused to forget. Even when it hurt."

Julien opened his suitcase. Pulled out a stack of postcards, edges worn soft by time and hope.

"I don't know if they're true," he said. "Some might be fiction."

"Truth is what you choose to remember," said the Emperor. "And what you give away."

He touched one of the postcards. It fluttered upward, then another, and another, until the air was full of them—dancing like leaves, scattering light. Some dissolved into flame. Others folded into birds. A few whispered as they flew, faint voices repeating names, places, fragments.

The Emperor extended a hand. In his palm was a key. Rusted, crooked, warm.

"This will open the door to the car that doesn't exist," he said. "You'll know it when you see it."

Julien took it.

When he looked up again, the Emperor was gone.

He stepped back through the mirror. The train resumed its rhythm—soft, steady, infinite. He returned to his seat in Car Seven, the key in his coat pocket, the name *Julien* quietly echoing in his chest.

And then, at the end of the train, he found it.

A door with no handle. Just a keyhole and a symbol: a cracked circle.

He inserted the key. Turned.

The door opened onto a single chair in an empty room. No windows. No lights.

But as he entered, the room changed.

Walls grew around him—soft green. A window appeared, cracked open to let in the scent of rain. A record spun on a dusty player. There was a mug on a desk. Still warm.

It was his room. Not one he'd remembered—but one he had clearly lived in. The marks on the doorframe. The photos taped to the mirror. A note pinned to the wall in handwriting he now recognized as his own:

> "If you're reading this, it means you made it back."

And then he saw the mirror.

This time, the reflection was whole.

He looked like Julien.

He looked like someone who had once stood in the rain, heart wide open, laughing.

He looked like someone who still could.

He sat in the chair.

Closed his eyes.

And for the first time in a long time, he *remembered*.

By: Alden Blake

The girl in the bookstore who read poems aloud when she thought no one was listening. The friend who painted stars on the ceiling of his first apartment. The morning he made pancakes from scratch and got every single one wrong—but they'd eaten them anyway, because they were laughing too hard to care.

He remembered dancing in a kitchen, holding hands with someone whose name came back like a breath: Elise.

He remembered joy.

It wasn't grand. It wasn't loud. It wasn't forever.

But it had *been*.

And that made it real.

When he opened his eyes, the room began to dissolve—gently, like mist rising off a field at dawn. The chair faded. The walls softened. The cracked circle on the door glowed once, then vanished.

Julien stood.

He was back in Car Seven.

The train moved on. It always would.

But now, he had a name.

A pocketful of postcards.

And a memory he had chosen to keep.

CHAPTER 9:
A NAME IN THE SMOKE

The first time he saw the name, it was spelled out in the curling grey smoke of a house fire on Wexley Street. It shimmered faintly above the scorched beams like a skywritten signature—*MILA*. Just that. Four letters, coiled and delicate, like the breath of something unseen.

He blinked. It was gone.

Firefighters are trained not to believe in ghosts. They are taught that smoke is chemistry and instinct and timing. That a name is just a trick of the eyes, or the heat, or the adrenaline.

But the second time, two weeks later, it appeared again—rising from the window of a burning nursery in a townhome on Cardamon Hill. This time, the smoke didn't drift lazily. It formed *MILA* with eerie precision, each letter distinct, unfurling in the same elegant, deliberate way. The same size. The same tilt.

Firefighter Lennox Harper stood outside the smoldering building with his mask in his hands, sweat pouring down his neck despite the snow swirling around him, and watched it vanish.

He didn't tell anyone. Not then.

But from that moment forward, the name followed him.

Every fire. Every call. No matter the street, the neighborhood, the scale of the disaster—*MILA* would be there, somewhere. In the plume from a burning attic. In the ghosting ash that rose from collapsed rafters. Once, even in the steam hissing up from a scorched bathtub, as if the smoke had found a new language in water.

He began to dread going in.

The others called it burnout. Lennox called it haunting.

And still, no child was ever found.

No child missing. No bodies. No reports of a girl named Mila. The name wasn't connected to any victim, any case, any family. It was as if she existed only in the smoke—and maybe in him.

He started carrying a notebook.

At first, it was just descriptions. Sketches. Times and dates. The way the letters curved like handwriting, sometimes upright, sometimes slanted. Then it became stranger. He began recording what he *felt* when he saw the name.

> "Today, the smoke smelled like violets and wet chalk. When I saw her name, I remembered the sound of windchimes."

> "Third fire this week. Her name in the hallway mirror, fogged like breath. Afterward, I felt like I'd forgotten something important—like waking from a dream you were supposed to finish."

> "MILA. Same as always. But today, I whispered it back. I think I heard a laugh."

He didn't tell the crew. You didn't survive years in this job by admitting you talked to the smoke.

Captain Ramírez, a skeptic to her bones, would've written it off as sleep deprivation or trauma. Lennox had known her long enough to predict the speech— take a week off, talk to someone, maybe look at retirement early. But that wasn't it. He *knew* it wasn't.

Mila had become more than a name. She was a presence now.

He began seeing her shadow in the corners of rooms that weren't burning. A flash of movement in the reflection of a window. Once, during a routine inspection, he opened a closet door and saw handprints in ash on the inside—small, like a child's.

Still, no reports. No leads. No answers.

But Lennox was used to silence. He'd spent most of his adult life in it.

He lived alone. No kids. No partner. His one-bedroom apartment above the laundromat was filled with the kind of quiet that seemed to hum when you turned the lights off. He didn't keep many pictures. One of his mother—gone now, lung cancer. One of the station crew, four years back, all grinning in gear. And one photo he'd never been able to explain.

It showed a little girl with dark hair and bright eyes, maybe four or five, laughing in a garden he didn't recognize.

There was no name written on the back. He had no idea where the picture had come from.

He kept it in his wallet anyway.

Some nights, after a hard call, he would take the photo out and look at it under the kitchen light. Just to remind himself he wasn't crazy.

Then came the fire on Holloway Drive.

It was supposed to be routine. A two-story bungalow. Faulty wiring. No one inside.

But as Lennox stepped through the blackened doorway, a wave of cold swept over him. Not heat. Not smoke. *Cold.* Like winter through a keyhole.

And there—above the collapsed staircase—was her name again.

MILA.

Only this time, it was more than just smoke.

The letters hung in the air like lace. Solid. Tangible. And behind them, the outline of something small moved. Darted. Hid.

He dropped his axe.

"Mila?" he called, not even thinking.

The air stilled. He could hear the crackle of flame behind the walls, the strain of beams above him. But all else was silent.

Then—barely above a whisper—he heard it.

"Yes."

He turned. The room was empty.

But when he looked down, he saw footprints in the ash. Small ones. Leading up the stairs.

He followed.

By: Alden Blake

Every instinct screamed at him to stop. The structure was compromised. The upper floor had already begun to give. But the footprints glowed faintly, like embers.

He climbed.

At the top, in what had once been a child's bedroom, the air was thick. The smoke curled around him, playful and strange.

And in the center of the room, standing barefoot in a circle of untouched floorboards, was a girl.

She looked just like the photo.

Dark hair. Bright eyes. A red ribbon in her braid.

"Mila?" he asked again, breath caught in his throat.

She nodded. "You remembered."

He opened his mouth. Closed it. How do you talk to a ghost? A hallucination? A child made of ash and memory?

"Who are you?" he asked.

"I'm the part you lost," she said.

The floor groaned. Sparks drifted upward. Lennox stepped closer.

"What do you mean?"

But she didn't answer. She only pointed—to the wall behind her.

There, scrawled in soot and shadow, was something new.

Not *MILA* this time.

LENNOX.

His own name.

It looked like a signature. Not smoke, but charcoal. Like something burned into the room long before today.

He stepped back.

The girl was gone.

The room was empty again.

And then, with a thunderous creak, the ceiling gave way.

They pulled him out twenty minutes later.

Bruised, coughing, alive.

He didn't tell them what he saw.

But when he got home that night, he opened his notebook and wrote:

By: Alden Blake

"Her name is Mila. And she is *mine*. Or maybe I am hers. I think I knew her once. Before the fire. Before the forgetting."

He looked again at the photo.

This time, there was writing on the back.

Not printed. Not penned. Scratched faintly in with something sharp.

Your daughter. Don't forget.

He couldn't sleep.

The photo now lay on the kitchen counter, illuminated by the amber flicker of the stovetop light—*Your daughter. Don't forget.* The message carved on the back in shaky, desperate lines had sent his thoughts spiraling. The words didn't feel metaphorical. They felt like a key. A warning. A plea.

But Lennox didn't have a daughter. He'd never been married, never been in one place long enough to build anything that lasted. At least... that's what he believed. That's what his memories told him.

But what if his memories were wrong?

He poured himself a glass of water and stared at the photo again. The child's face felt impossibly familiar now. Not just because he'd stared at it so often—but because something deep inside him recognized her. The way her eyes tilted up when she laughed. The curl of her lip. The same shade of copper in her hair he used to see in the mirror before the grey took over.

He picked up the photo. Turned it over again. Ran his fingers across the back.

Your daughter.

"Mila," he said softly.

He'd known the name. Before the fires. Long before.

A memory surfaced, sudden and vivid: a park bench beneath an elm tree. A woman beside him, sketching leaves in a notebook. Her hand resting on her stomach.

"What if it's a girl?" she had asked.

"I like the name Mila," he'd said, surprising even himself.

The memory was gone as quickly as it came.

His hands trembled. He picked up his phone. Began to dig.

He didn't know what he was looking for. Birth records? Obituaries? News reports? *Anything.*

He started with the name: **Mila Harper**. Nothing. A few social media accounts. One girl who reviewed YA novels on YouTube. No one who matched.

By: Alden Blake

He tried **Mila + Fire**. That turned up several tragic headlines—none local. None recent.

Then, on a whim, he searched **Mila + Elmfield**—the name of the park from the flickering memory.

One hit.

A fire. Sixteen years ago. A small apartment complex. Faulty stove. Two deaths. One child unaccounted for.

He clicked the link. The article was archived, yellowed with digital age. No photos, no video. Just a few paragraphs.

> *June 4th, 2009 – A fire broke out late Thursday evening at the Elmfield Terrace Apartments. Two adults were found deceased inside. A child, Mila Lane, age five, was listed as missing and presumed dead. Officials noted difficulty in identifying remains due to extensive damage. No body recovered. Investigation closed.*

Lane.

His breath caught.

He knew that name. *Eva Lane.*

He opened another tab. Typed faster now: **Eva Lane + Lennox Harper.**

It took longer, but he found it. An old police blotter. Domestic disturbance report. Nothing charged. Just a name, an address, and a note:

> *Ex-partner refused to vacate premises. Officer present to retrieve belongings. No children mentioned at the scene.*

He sat back in the chair.

Eva Lane. His ex.

The woman from the bench. The one who used to sketch leaves and hum jazz standards under her breath. The one who moved out while he was on a long shift and left no note. The one he hadn't thought about in over a decade—until now.

She'd been pregnant when she left.

He stood up, dizzy.

"Mila," he whispered again.

The fires. The name. The photo. The memory.

He grabbed his coat.

At the station the next morning, he arrived early. Before the others. Before the coffee was even brewing.

He headed straight for the archives.

By: Alden Blake

Captain Ramírez had always hated paper, but the department's older records still lived in a backroom—scorched and curling at the corners. Most never digitized. Fires that happened before smartphones made tragedy shareable.

He found the Elmfield fire folder in a warped filing cabinet labeled *2009–2011: CLOSED*.

It contained three sheets of paper and a blurry, black-and-white photo of a scorched doll.

> Victims: Eva Lane (29), Samuel Keller (32)
> Child listed: Mila Lane (5) – *unrecovered*

He turned the page. A handwritten note from the responding officer.

> *Room contained toys, clothes. Evidence of child's presence. No visual confirmation during search. Presumed perished due to severity of blaze. No remains found.*

Lennox closed the folder, heart pounding.

Something was wrong.

There was no mention of *him*. No mention that *he* might have been Mila's father. No DNA request. No next-of-kin notification. Eva had vanished from his life like a page torn from a book—and the fire had erased the rest.

He stared at the name again. *Mila Lane.*

Why Lane? Why not Harper?

Because Eva didn't want him involved. Because she had left before the baby came. Because she never told him.

He sat in the archive room for a long time, the folder in his lap, the smell of old paper and faint smoke clinging to the air.

When the others began arriving, he slipped out.

That night, he drove to Elmfield Terrace.

The apartment complex was still there. Rebuilt. Sleeker now, with a new name: *The Terraces at Elmfield Ridge*. Nothing of the old brick façade remained. But Lennox recognized the tree—the great elm in the middle of the courtyard, stubborn and vast, untouched by fire or time.

He sat beneath it.

Closed his eyes.

Tried to remember.

There had been laughter. Crayons. A chalk mural of the sun on the sidewalk. He remembered a small pair of sneakers on the porch, red with white laces. He remembered telling someone a story—something

By: Alden Blake

about a lion and a storm—and hearing a giggle that made his chest ache.

He remembered love.

And he remembered losing it.

Lennox opened his eyes.

Across the courtyard, faint and flickering like a mirage, he saw smoke rise from a second-floor window.

Just a curl. Just a wisp.

And in it—once again—her name.

MILA.

He stood. Walked toward the building.

The smoke vanished.

But at his feet, in the patchy grass near the elm, he saw something buried.

He knelt. Dug gently with his fingers until they scraped metal.

A charm bracelet. Burnt. Bent.

It had three charms: a heart, a lion, and the letter *M*.

He held it in his hand, trembling.

This was real.

She had been real.

She might *still* be real.

Somewhere between memory and flame.

And he was going to find her.

The bracelet sat in his palm like a relic—burnt, warped, impossibly light. He traced the lion charm with his thumb, remembering now with a clarity that didn't feel earned, like the memory had been loaned to him from someone else's dream.

He hadn't just known her name. He had *given* it to her.

Mila.

The name that had haunted him, spelled itself in every column of smoke, whispered itself into the folds of his brain like a song he once knew by heart.

He should have remembered her sooner.

But grief, it turned out, was not always thunderous. Sometimes it was slow and soft and smoky, folding itself into the corners of a life, reshaping silence into something survivable. He hadn't forgotten Mila all at once. He'd simply let time take her, inch by inch, smudging her name until all he was left with was the shape of something missing.

By: Alden Blake

Now she was everywhere.

In dreams. In fires. In fogged mirrors and half-remembered melodies. She had found her way back to him through ash and flame, like some ember that refused to go out.

But why now?

Why after all these years?

He returned to the site again the next day. Then the next. Sometimes he brought flowers. Sometimes the bracelet. Once, he just sat and said her name aloud until the sun went down.

Nothing happened. No smoke. No ghost. Just the creak of branches above him and the soft rattle of wind through brittle leaves.

And yet he felt watched.

Not by something sinister. Not even by something sad. But by something *waiting*.

A week later, he knocked on the door of the only person still alive who might know the truth.

Mrs. Callahan had been Eva's neighbor back then. She now lived in a retirement village on the edge of town, where the hallways smelled like paper towels and boiled tea. She didn't recognize Lennox at first, but when he said "Eva Lane," she blinked twice and sat down hard in a wicker chair.

"She was lovely," the old woman said. "Quiet. Artistic. Kept to herself after the baby."

"So Mila was real," he said.

"Oh yes," she said softly. "The sweetest girl. Big eyes. Loved lions. Always drew them in chalk on the sidewalk."

Lennox felt his throat close.

"She died in the fire," he said, though it came out as a question.

Mrs. Callahan didn't answer right away. She looked out the window instead.

"They never found her," she said finally. "But Eva used to say—when she was still here—that Mila was a dream. Not a girl. A dream she had so often it became real to her. Said she wasn't sure if Mila had ever really been born. Or if she'd lost her before the world ever got to meet her."

"What do you mean?"

Mrs. Callahan turned to him. Her eyes were pale and full of rustling thoughts.

"I mean Eva believed she carried Mila... but that the fire came before she had the chance to hold her. And after that, she just kept seeing her. Hearing her. Like the child had slipped through into smoke instead of air."

That night, Lennox stood outside a burning warehouse off Grand Avenue. Arson, they said. No casualties. Just property loss.

But the moment he stepped into the blackened hallway, the smoke curled around him like a whisper.

MILA.

He didn't run. He didn't look away.

He followed.

Down the corridor. Up the stairs. Into a room that should've been empty.

But in the center, where the roof had caved in to moonlight, stood a figure.

Not a child.

A girl now. Maybe seventeen. The same hair. The same eyes. Taller. But still her.

Still Mila.

He said her name.

She turned.

"I'm not supposed to exist," she said, voice thin as wind.

"But you do," he whispered.

She looked at her hands, then back at him. "Not always. Only when you remember."

He stepped closer. "I tried to. I swear."

"I know."

Silence fell between them.

"I don't know what's real anymore," he admitted.

"That's not the same as forgetting."

She smiled.

And in the smoke behind her, he saw flashes of chalk drawings. A lion. A woman's laughter. A park bench. A sunlit hallway. A crib that never held a name.

Grief is a fog, she seemed to say. It reshapes the house but keeps the foundation.

He reached out.

But she was already gone.

They found him the next morning, alone in the ruins of the warehouse, sitting cross-legged on the ash-covered floor. His coat was singed. His hands were blackened. But he was unhurt.

He said nothing to the crew. Not about the girl. Not about her name.

But that night, he returned home, opened his notebook, and wrote:

> "You were real, even if the world forgot. Even if I did. You were real because I remember how you laughed when I made the lion voice. Because I kept your photo when I didn't know why. Because smoke carried your name back to me like a message I was too broken to read."

He folded the page and placed it with the bracelet in a small tin box.

Then he lit a single match.

Held it just long enough to see its shape.

And blew it out.

Weeks passed.

The fires stopped spelling her name.

He still looked, of course. Out of habit. Out of hope.

But the smoke was just smoke again. Wild. Random. Without language.

Still, he felt lighter.

Not whole. But no longer hollow.

Sometimes he swore he heard footsteps in his apartment at night. Barefoot. Small. A creak in the hall where there shouldn't be one. Once, the smell of chalk and violets after he'd returned from a shift.

Sometimes he'd whisper, *Mila,* into the dark.

Sometimes the dark whispered back.

One day, he returned to the elm tree at Elmfield. Sat beneath it in silence.

Above him, the branches swayed gently.

And carved into the bark, just faint enough to miss if you weren't looking, were the words:

Thank you for remembering.

He smiled.

And for the first time in a long time, he wept.

By: Alden Blake

CHAPTER 10:
THE LAST EMPEROR OF GLADNESS

The city had been drained of color long before it forgot how to feel.

It began with the banning of grief. Officials said it was corrosive. Unproductive. A burden on the collective psyche. Grief pulled people from their jobs, their families, their assigned societal functions. And so they outlawed mourning—not suddenly, but in increments: first funeral gatherings, then elegies, then tears in public spaces. Therapists were replaced with *Emotive Neutralization Agents*, whose job was to administer correction when someone broke the rules.

Soon after, joy followed.

Laughter was too volatile, too disruptive. Smiles suggested internal states that could not be monitored.

Romance led to heartbreak, and heartbreak to despair. Love, the officials decided, was an illogical loyalty to impermanent things.

By the time the last billboard was torn down—an old advertisement featuring a couple dancing in the rain— no one remembered why people had ever wanted to feel at all.

Children were raised with sensory conditioning, their emotional spectrums dulled to grayscale. Schools taught logic, compliance, and useful historical omissions. Art was relegated to functional design; music to factory alerts. Facial expressions were discouraged unless performed as part of a required protocol.

The city was safe. Clean. Efficient.

It was also utterly, crushingly silent.

And yet... something was happening.

Small things. Impossible things.

Someone had drawn a smiley face on a train window in the condensation. A forbidden word—*gladness*— had been found scrawled in chalk outside a school. A bouquet of wildflowers had appeared on the steps of City Hall. They had no scent—scent was illegal—but they *looked* like joy.

The officials called it *The Gladness Anomaly*.

By: Alden Blake

The public called it nothing. No one was supposed to speak of it.

But still, rumors spread.

They said he was real. The man who smiled in the rain. Who wore a paper crown and danced in abandoned plazas. The one who spoke not in lectures, but in laughter. Who left footprints in the paint of old murals and stories under park benches.

They called him **The Last Emperor of Gladness**.

Marin had never cried. Not because she didn't want to—but because she didn't know how.

She had seen someone do it once. A boy in her orientation cohort. He had made a sound—wet, guttural—and then just... leaked. His face twisted, his shoulders shook. She had watched in awe, unsure whether it was pain or transformation. They took him away before she could ask.

She was seventeen now. Lived in Sector D, Block 14. Worked in Cataloging, Tier II. Her days were filled with data entry and code-stamping, and her evenings with silence. She didn't mind. She had been trained not to.

But sometimes... sometimes she dreamed.

Not sanctioned dreams—those were scrubbed each morning with cognitive routines. But strange dreams. Wild ones. A man in a tattered robe made of newspaper. A throne of umbrellas. A voice that echoed like laughter inside an empty hall.

"You have to remember," the dream man always said. "You were born for joy."

She never told anyone.

Not even when she found the coin.

It was lying on the sidewalk outside her block one morning. Not an official token—just a small circle of copper with a crude smiling face carved into one side. On the back: *Rain is just sky laughter.*

It made no sense. And yet she kept it.

Hid it behind a vent in her wall.

She began to notice more signs.

A folded paper crown left on a park bench. A recording chip labeled *DO NOT LISTEN* that played a faint melody before self-erasing. A red balloon floating outside her work terminal, drifting against all wind patterns.

Each time, she felt... something.

A pull. A flicker.

By: Alden Blake

A possibility.

One evening, walking home after a systems audit, Marin saw the word again—written in melted candle wax across the pavement in front of the Civic Tower.

GLADNESS

She stopped.

It pulsed faintly in the fading light, like a secret trying to breathe.

Around her, other pedestrians walked by without looking. Whether they didn't see it or had trained themselves not to, she couldn't tell. But none reacted. None slowed.

She bent down. Touched it.

Warm.

She looked up. A man was watching her from across the plaza.

He wore a long coat patched with scraps of cloth and ribbons. His face was mostly hidden, but his eyes were impossibly kind. And on his head sat a fragile, crumpled paper crown.

He raised one hand—not in warning, but in invitation.

Then turned and walked away.

She followed.

They moved through side streets and back alleys, past shuttered cafés and forgotten fountains, until they reached the old library. It had been closed for years, deemed "emotionally hazardous" due to the presence of unredacted fiction. No one went inside anymore.

But the man pushed open the door.

Inside, it was not empty.

Candles burned in old bottles. Music—soft and defiant—played from a wind-up record player. People sat in quiet circles, reading aloud from banned pages, painting symbols on scraps of cloth, sharing food that hadn't been synthetically approved.

And on the far wall, painted in golden letters, were the words:

> *We are not broken. We are paused.*
> *The Last Emperor lives in every dream unreported.*
> *Joy will return.*

The man turned to her. Removed his crown.

He was older than she expected. Not a ghost. Not a legend.

Just a man with eyes full of remembered color.

By: Alden Blake

"You found the coin," he said.

She nodded.

"Then you're ready."

"For what?"

He smiled.

"For the rebellion of gladness."

The rebellion didn't move in thunder. It moved in whispers, gestures, and the quiet handing off of forbidden memories.

Marin learned quickly: the Emperor was not a man, not really. He was an idea—a shared hallucination that kept evolving each time someone dared to remember what joy once felt like. The man she'd followed, whose name was Jasper, had worn the paper crown for thirteen years. Before him, it had been an old painter. Before that, a child. The Emperor was a rotating flame passed from hand to hand.

"No one can be glad forever," Jasper told her. "But anyone can guard the ember for a while."

In a back room of the ruined library, beneath a skylight covered in ivy, they kept a *Vault of Remembered Things*—items banned or erased by the Regime. Marin wandered the shelves, touching memories she'd never had: a baby shoe with tiny stars drawn on the sole. A cassette labeled "Her Laugh,

August 3rd." A cracked teacup with initials carved into the base. A painting of a red balloon in a yellow sky.

The objects hummed faintly, as if still tethered to the people who had once loved them.

One night, Marin was cataloging recovered artifacts when a man limped in through the back door. His uniform marked him as a firefighter—one of the few state jobs still held by individuals rather than drones.

He placed something on the table.

A soot-covered bracelet.

"She kept appearing in the smoke," he said quietly. "A name. A face. I didn't know if she was real until I started remembering differently."

He looked up. His eyes were tired but unguarded.

"I think she was someone I forgot to grieve."

Marin said nothing. Just reached out and gently closed his hand around the bracelet again.

"Then maybe now," she whispered, "you can."

He left before dawn.

His story stayed behind.

By: Alden Blake

Later that week, a composer came into the library. Older. Unshaven. His coat smelled like rust and coffee grounds.

He sat down at the cracked piano in the reading room and played a single melody—slow, searching, broken in parts.

"It came from a dream," he murmured when Marin approached. "I've been chasing it most of my life. I used to think it belonged to someone I lost. But I think now... it belongs to everyone who forgot how to feel."

The melody made something inside Marin ache. Not in pain—but in recognition.

She sat beside him as he played it again.

By the fourth repetition, she was humming along.

The rebellion had no manifesto. Its only creed was this: *Remember what they told you to forget.*

Some remembered through music.

Others through painting, like the street artist who arrived covered in charcoal and streaked paint. He said little, but once left behind a sketchbook filled with faces of strangers—some missing, some imagined, some drawn so vividly they seemed alive.

Marin recognized one face: a woman with kind eyes and a paper crown, drawn in watercolors and light.

"She was the first," Jasper said. "Or maybe just the first to smile without flinching."

In another drawing, a boy stood in the rain, holding up a newspaper crown as if it could stop the sky. Below it, a handwritten caption: *The Paper City never burned.*

One night, Marin dreamed of a train again.

But this time, she was on board.

She walked its endless corridors as passengers stared blankly ahead. Each seat bore a plaque: *Subject resigned to memory void.* But one passenger, near the back, was different. He wrote postcards to himself with shaking hands, each one a desperate attempt to recall something lost.

He looked up at her.

"They took the yesterday from me," he said. "But I still remember a smile on a platform. Might've been mine. Might've been hers."

She tried to speak, but the dream dissolved into smoke.

By: Alden Blake

When she woke, she could still feel the ink of his postcards on her palms.

Jasper explained that dreams were their most powerful currency.

"The mind," he said, "is the last free country."

Each recovered memory—each illicit emotion—was a crack in the city's immaculate shell.

Sometimes those cracks widened.

A child at a state school laughed aloud during a presentation. No one knew why. But for a moment, the whole classroom stilled—something like wonder creeping into their carefully trained expressions.

In a manufacturing zone, an engineer played a forbidden song on a circuit board. Just three notes, looped quietly, but it made the machines hum in harmony instead of monotony.

And once, someone projected a hologram over the Civic Tower—a brief, looping video of people dancing in slow motion. Old people, children, lovers, friends.

They didn't smile.

They *beamed*.

The Regime scrubbed it within minutes. But not before thousands saw it.

Marin was one of them.

She cried for the first time that night. No sobs. No shaking. Just tears—slow, astonished.

She didn't want them to stop.

Jasper grew weaker. Some said the longer you wore the crown, the more it stole from you—like carrying a bright flame in your chest that eventually burned you hollow.

Before he stepped down, he told Marin something she would carry forever.

"Joy isn't just feeling good. It's knowing the world can be beautiful even when it isn't. It's defiance. It's remembering that your soul belongs to you."

He handed her the crown—not as a burden, but as a torch.

"Keep it safe," he said. "Or pass it on. The Emperor doesn't have to rule. He just has to remind."

The night she took the paper crown, Marin stood on the roof of the old library, wind tugging at her coat.

By: Alden Blake

Below, the city glowed with sterile lights and efficient silence.

But behind her, in the shelter of books and memory and reclaimed dreams, something real was growing.

Not a rebellion.

A revival.

And somewhere in the city, she felt them all:

—The boy who had built a world of paper and believed in an emperor.

—The waitress who mistook every stranger for someone she loved and was never quite wrong.

—The child who drew lions in chalk and whispered her name into smoke.

—The man writing himself back into existence, one postcard at a time.

—The composer who heard music in grief.

—The painter who saw people no one else noticed.

—The merchant who searched for the hour of gladness.

—And the last laugh echoing in an empty theater, reminding the walls that they had once held joy.

They were all still here.

Waiting. Waking. Remembering.

And now, so was she.

They said he wore a crown made of newsprint, soft with rain and creased at the edges.

They said he once stood at the edge of the Civic Tower during a thunderstorm, arms outstretched, smiling as lightning forked through the clouds.

They said he could coax laughter from a room with a single look.

They said he had a name, but no one agreed on what it was. Some believed he'd never had one. Others claimed he'd given it away long ago, traded it for the memory of someone else's happiest day.

But more than anything, they said this:

He reminded people what it felt like to be glad.

The rebellion didn't march.

It didn't chant or burn or riot.

It whispered.

It sang in stairwells. It scribbled messages in sidewalk chalk. It left notes inside hollow trees and paper crowns beneath benches. It spread through dreams— unmapped, unregulated. It gathered in the warmth of

By: Alden Blake

kitchens, in the corners of empty art museums, in broken plazas where people once danced.

And through it all, *The Emperor* lingered—not always seen, not always mentioned, but always known.

Children began to draw him in the margins of their schoolbooks: a tall figure in mismatched boots, with eyes like upside-down commas and a crown that changed shape depending on who described it.

Some called him a ghost. Others, a guardian. A few believed he was just a story—a trick of collective memory, pieced together from fragments of longing.

But Marin knew better.

The Emperor was real.

Even if he wasn't one person. Even if he didn't always have a body. He was real the way laughter is real, the way warmth spreads from hand to hand, the way one shared glance can carry a thousand forgotten things.

She wore the paper crown sometimes. Not always. Not as a claim to power, but as a signal—one that said: *I remember, and I want you to remember too.*

In Sector B, someone rewired a city terminal to play forbidden music when touched. Passersby would hear three seconds of a melody before it vanished. Those three seconds were enough to make them pause. Sometimes enough to make them weep.

In Sector J, the phrase "Where the dandelions grow" was found etched into a transit wall. No one knew who wrote it, but it began appearing in more places— along stair railings, inside elevator panels, behind restroom mirrors. It became a sort of code: a memory of something soft, something growing.

And in the sky above the west plaza, a hologram briefly flickered: a city made of folded newspaper, glowing from within. It lasted only seven seconds. Long enough for a small crowd to gather and stare upward, their faces unguarded for the first time in years.

One girl whispered: "It's beautiful."

No one corrected her.

The Regime responded as they always had: with silencing.

Propaganda drones broadcast reminders of *Emotional Containment Law 3.4.*

Informants were rewarded for reporting "joy-based infractions."

Libraries were scanned. Playgrounds were closed. Rain was chemically thickened to prevent puddles.

By: Alden Blake

But it didn't matter anymore.

The cracks had widened too far.

Once a person remembered how to feel, they could not *un*-remember. They might hide it, repress it, even fear it—but it was there, buried like spring beneath frost.

And The Emperor was everywhere.

Not just in rumors, but in reflections. In the man who painted joy on condemned buildings. In the woman who recited poetry to birds. In the old comedian who left punchlines in envelopes around the city. In the composer who scattered his final notes like seeds into the wind.

And in Marin.

Especially Marin.

She stood one evening at the train station—Platform 9, long disused.

It was raining softly, the kind of rain that felt like memory.

She wore the crown—not the same one Jasper gave her, but a new one she'd made from pages of an old children's book. It had pictures of oceans and stars.

A boy approached. Maybe eight years old. Holding a postcard. The name field was blank.

"I think this was meant for you," he said.

She turned it over. The message read:

> *I remember the day we laughed for no reason. It was the best day. I hope it wasn't a dream.*

She knelt beside the boy.

"What's your name?" she asked.

He looked around, uncertain.

"I... don't know anymore."

She smiled.

"Maybe that's okay. Maybe you're still choosing."

He smiled back.

Later, she would meet others who had once appeared only in stories.

A waitress with kind eyes who asked if she looked familiar.

A firefighter who still smelled faintly of ash, cradling a new bracelet in his palm.

By: Alden Blake

A man who played a melody no one could name but everyone remembered.

Each encounter was brief. Fleeting. Like crossing paths in a dream.

But they were real.

And they carried something with them—a hush, a warmth, a thread pulled from a tapestry long thought lost.

The city changed slowly.

Not in revolution, but in resonance.

An old theater reopened—not officially, but in secret, its stage lit by candles and voices.

A painter began teaching children how to draw what they felt, not what they saw.

And somewhere deep in the archives, someone found a document with the word "gladness" still intact. They didn't report it. They copied it onto a thousand slips of paper and released them into the wind.

People collected them like wishes.

Marin never declared herself the Emperor.

She didn't have to.

Others wore the crown in her absence. Some for a day, some for years. It passed between rebels like fire in a paper lantern—fragile, luminous, unbroken by the dark.

In time, the question of whether he'd ever existed stopped mattering.

Because the truth was this:

He always had.

And always would.

Wherever someone chose joy over fear. Wherever someone laughed when they weren't supposed to. Wherever someone remembered a melody, a face, a name they'd once loved.

The Emperor lived.

Not as a ruler.

But as a reminder.

That gladness—true, defiant, impossible gladness—could never be outlawed.

The Quiet Light

The city had changed, but not in the ways the Regime had feared. It did not fall in a blaze of rebellion or thunderous revolt. Instead, it shifted like a tide pulling back, revealing something that had always been there beneath the surface—a fragile, flickering light that no order could snuff out.

Marin stood by the window of the old library, now a sanctuary for the memories the world tried to erase. Outside, the rain tapped gently against the glass, a soft symphony of persistence. It reminded her of something long ago, a boy with a paper city, a melody that once belonged to a dream, a laugh echoing in an empty theater. These fragments, scattered like stars, had woven themselves into the quiet fabric of the world.

Joy was not a grand monument to be built or destroyed. It was a whisper carried in the wind, a secret shared between strangers, a memory breathed back to life in the dark. It was the smallest gesture—a hand held when no one was watching, a song hummed softly in the night, a name spoken aloud after years of silence.

Memory was both blessing and burden. It held the power to wound and to heal. To forget was to lose a part of oneself, but to remember was to reclaim a piece of the soul. The stories of the last Emperor, the boy who built worlds, the firefighter who saw names in smoke—they were all echoes of this truth: that we are defined by what we hold in our hearts, even when the world tells us to let go.

Marin traced her fingers over the paper crown resting beside her—a symbol not of power, but of hope. It was worn and creased, fragile as the emotions it represented, yet in its delicate folds lived the strength to defy a world grown cold.

She thought of the faces she had met—each one a thread in the tapestry of rebellion, each one carrying a spark that refused to be extinguished. Together, they were not just survivors. They were keepers of the ember, guardians of gladness in a world that tried to banish it.

The last Emperor was not a single man, but a chorus of voices, a constellation of memories, a living poem written by countless hands. And as long as even one soul dared to remember, to feel, to hope—the Emperor would never truly be gone.

Because joy, in all its messy, fleeting beauty, was what made them human.

And that was a truth no crown could ever take away.

The rain slowed, and for a moment, the city seemed to hold its breath—waiting, watching, remembering.

And somewhere deep inside, a quiet light began to glow.

By: Alden Blake

Conclusion

J oy is a fragile thing.
   A whisper caught between pages,
   a breath held in a moment just before dawn,
a flicker of warmth beneath the cold skin of the
world.

It slips through fingers like dust,
 yet it lingers in corners unseen,
 in the spaces between heartbeats,
 where memory and longing entwine.

Across ten stories, ten lives,
 we traced its light—
 from a boy's paper city,
 to a café filled with ghosts of second chances,
 to melodies heard only in dreams,
 to laughter lost and found in empty theaters,
 to shadows sketched with charcoal and hope.

We walked through gardens where dandelions grow
wild,

rode trains that forgot their passengers,
watched smoke curl around names never spoken
aloud,
and finally, stood beneath the crown of a last
emperor,
a figure both real and imagined—
a guardian of what was, and what could still be.

What binds these tales is not place, nor time,
but the quiet pulse beneath them all—
the stubborn insistence of joy
to survive, to resist,
even when the world grows cold and dark.

Joy is rebellion.
A refusal to be erased,
a song sung softly in a city silenced,
a smile offered to the rain.

It is both delicate and fierce—
a paper crown soaked through by storms,
yet unyielding in its shape.

To remember joy is to remember ourselves—
the messy, radiant humanity beneath the surface.
To hold onto it is to carry a flame
against the shadows that would snuff it out.

The Last Emperor of Gladness is not a man,
but a symbol—a flicker, a flame,
a testament to the enduring power of light
in the deepest night.

By: Alden Blake

In these stories, we find the quiet courage to feel,
to laugh, to mourn, to hope.
We find that joy, though fragile,
is never truly lost—
only waiting, waiting for a hand to lift it up again.

And so, in the end, it is this—
the unbreakable thread of joy—
that connects us all.

A crown of paper and light,
passed from heart to heart,
across the fragile spaces of memory,
reminding us that even in a world of shadows,
gladness can live.

"Joy is the quiet rebellion of the human spirit—a light that no darkness can truly extinguish."
— Alden Blake

The End

Made in the USA
Columbia, SC
22 May 2025

58311786R00102